I0531608

Storylandia

The Wapshott Journal of Fiction

Issue 11

The Wapshott Press

Storylandia, Issue 11, The Wapshott Journal of Fiction, ISSN 1947-5349, ISBN 978-0-9848325-9-0, is published at intervals by the Wapshott Press, PO Box 31513, Los Angeles, California, 90031-0513, telephone 323-201-7147. All correspondence can be sent The Wapshott Press, PO Box 31513, LA CA 90031-0513. Visit our website at www. WapshottPress.com This work is copyright © 2013 by Storylandia. The Wapshott Journal of Fiction, Los Angeles, California. "Dr. Hackenbush Gets a Clue" is copyright © 2013 Ginger Mayerson and is reprinted here with the copyright owner's permission. Copyright for the cover artwork is held by the artist and is reprinted here with the copyright owner's permission.

Storylandia is always seeking quality original short stories, novelettes, and novellas. Please have a look at our submission guidelines at www.Storylandia.WapshottPress. com or email the editor at editor@wapshottpress.com

Many thanks to Nancy Lilly and Kathleen Warner for the proofreads and editorial support.

Cover: "Macarthur Park," by Justefrain, WikiMedia, 2009

Storylandia

The Wapshott Journal of Fiction

Founded in 2009

Issue 11, Autumn 2013

Edited by Ginger Mayerson

Table of Contents

Ginger Mayerson

Dr. Hackenbush Gets a Clue

1987

Some nights are really good... including the audience or lack of one. Mabel Hackenbush, fronting *Dr. Hackenbush and her Orchestra*, was having such a night. Ross on drums, Cody Cole on bass and Phil Noyes on guitar were playing as if they were born to play those instruments. Her dance partner, Shorty Smith, was dancing with inspiration and with Hackenbush, possibly more with inspiration since Hackenbush was merely a good dancer, not an inspired one. She was a better singer, and that night she was a great singer because she had nothing to lose: there was no audience to cater to, there was only the irritated club owner and the bar staff that looking half asleep. Or possibly they were just poleaxed with awe at this incredible, unrestrained performance that, to the unenlightened, might sound more like a no-holds-barred jam session, but was in fact five artists so caught up in the moment they–

And then halfway through the next to the last set thirty thirsty patrons poured in and put a serious damper on the band's enthusiasm. Civilians, they called them, dilettantes on the make, and more interested in each other than the music. That was okay. The Coral Cave wasn't a hardcore jazz club; it promoted itself as having tasteful music and tasty drinks. So the band became a tasteful accompaniment to a bunch of overdressed, emaciated, jittery-looking lounge lizards sucking down overpriced rum-laced fruit juice decorated with little paper umbrellas. As long as the band and Shorty were getting paid, Hackenbush wouldn't annoy the creepy patrons as they parted with the money that would eventually find its way into the band's bank accounts. This was her truce with and understanding of capitalism, as long as she didn't have to tolerate it too often. She figured the night would come out on the positive side because they got a good, free dinner and had two and a half smoking sets before they had to come back to earth.

In a way, Hackenbush was relieved they finally had a crowd. She hated to see a club, even one as badly situated and run as the Coral Cave, fail in Los Angeles, which—in her opinion—could never have too many clubs, even if she wasn't working in all of them. She was, in fact, impressed that anyone was in the Coral Cave at 11:30 PM on a Monday night and this close to Westlake's Macarthur Park, which had recently become even more the place to buy drugs in Los Angeles. Most nights, and some days, cars ranging from wrecks to new BMWs were pulling up on the south side of the park to make a buy. There was lots and lots of cocaine in LA lately, and there were more than enough buyers. Money and drugs brought violence, and the nighttime park was filled with shadows with unknown intentions. Not that any sane person went into Macarthur Park after dark—Hackenbush never went into it even during the day—

it was what spilled over into other blocks around it that was worrisome.

That was the gossip Hackenbush heard from her friends who still worked the occasional temp job in that neighborhood. Anna Kodaly had originally opened Temporary Insanity in a building just east of the park on Sixth Street, but moved over two miles west of it on Wilshire as soon as she could afford to do so. And Anna was tough, but not even she and her artist temps could raise the tone of that neighborhood. There was a pall of stress and despair over the whole area. Hackenbush wondered how any art was made at Otis Art Institute on the northwest corner of Wilshire and South Park View Street, but maybe the students just used the vibe as something to push against and made art anyway.

At the moment, Hackenbush was making a living as a musician and loving it. She and the band had four nights at the Lotus Room at the New Hotel Watenabe in Little Tokyo and enough casuals and gigs like the Coral Cave to stay solvent. Not that she didn't love Anna and wasn't grateful for all the temp gigs Anna got her that tided her over the thin spots, but she was so much happier this way.

Guitarist Phil, leaned over after the break tune and asked in an undertone, "Isn't that your old pal Mr. Bob Jones X over there?"

Setting her baritone ukulele in its stand, Hackenbush glanced into Phil's sweaty pasty white face and thought for the nth time he should smoke less and get out in the sun more. She opened her compact to check her lip gloss and caught sight of her own damp and pasty white face and thought she should smoke less and get out in the sun more. She lit a cigarette to underscore this thought and wondered why Phil was whispering to her about a guy on the other side of a noisy club when there was no way the guy could hear him. On the other hand, the former coke-dealing scum, Mr. X, self-rechristened as Bob Jones, was a scary guy and deeply loathed by Hackenbush, the band and all right-thinking people. It helped a little to think of him as Mr. Bob Jones X, incorporating the past into the present with a potent reminder that under that Armani suit there was a conglomeration of idiocy, violence and wastefulness that a name change and stellar tailoring could never completely dispel. In the old days, when he was a scruffy, coked-out white boy thug with no guts, they could almost tolerate him. He'd had an embarrassing crush on Hackenbush in those days, and to demonstrate his devotion, he'd comped her into an embarrassing coke habit her friends had to help her shake. Lately BJX had become, well, affluent and successful in "import/export" or so he said, and with success he'd become frightening. He'd gotten his hooks in Hackenbush's pal Lola Rae and getting her away from him and off drugs had nearly killed them all. Not that BJX threatened them; he'd thrown Lola away like a candy wrapper, but getting Lola off coke, with no rehab, just tough love and chicken soup and friends sitting with her in shifts 24/7 until she was straight enough to see what a narrow escape she'd had, that was what nearly killed them all. In these years when Nancy Reagan wanted mere humans addicted to the most powerful drugs on earth to just say no, there were no facilities available to help those who'd said yes to change their minds and their lives. Lola had been lucky to have friends like Hackenbush, the band, Anna Kodaly, and a dozen other artists who loved her enough to fight for her; the morgue and skid row were full of bodies that weren't so lucky.

"Hm. Know the guy with him?"

Leaning forward to ask his question, the drummer's big frame blocked a stage light and formed a nimbus around his head and shoulders. Nearly blinded by the glare off Ross' chocolate brown bald head, Hackenbush shielded her eyes. Ross was looking at her, but she knew he too was wondering about the overdressed Latino guy with BJX.

Hackenbush shook her head, and looked at natty Cody Cole, who didn't sweat much and never seemed to have a hair or seam out of place. He was a little lighter and shorter than Ross, and dressed to suit his café au lait good looks and wiry build. "What's he doing here, Hackenbush?" he asked in a normal tone of voice.

"I dunno, I didn't ask him," she snapped, and then lowered her voice. "This is his kind of crowd now, I think, lots of upper middle class money, ready to spend it on drugs..."

"And drinks and eats," Shorty put in, nodding in the direction of the mobbed bar and rushing wait staff. They couldn't see it, but they could hear through the swinging doors that the kitchen was jumpin' behind them.

"Speaking of, I'm dying of thirst." Hackenbush stalked off to get some non-alcoholic fruit juice. "Make that two, please," she said to the bartender, noticing Shorty beside her. "What do you think, pal?" she asked her dance partner.

Shorty pushed his cherubic jet ringlets off his glowing ivory forehead. Sweaty and pasty could never be applied to the delicate-looking, but tough as nails dancer, because he didn't smoke and he got more exercise than, well, all of them put together. He shrugged at her question and gave her his trademark grimace: a smile on the left side of his face and a frown on the right. Marcel Marceau had nothing on Shorty Smith, Hackenbush was sure of that.

It was possible Mr. Bob Jones X was in the Coral Cave that night with the jittery jeweled horde because Hackenbush was there. She was the one that got away, the one he couldn't ruin with drugs, and the one whose friends—Ross, Cody, Phil and Shorty—had chased him off with irony and kept him at bay with scorn. BJX had also been politely banned from the Lotus Room. Wang, the bartender, was a black belt in irony and scorn, and Mr. Tanaka himself had had firm, but pleasant and effective, words with BJX, who henceforth stayed the hell out of the Lotus Room. Mr. Tanaka was shorter than Hackenbush and Shorty, but he was a force unto himself and in his quiet way kept peace and order in the New Watanabe Hotel.

So, a slightly shady, but very public venue like the Coral Cave was where BJX could annoy Hackenbush with a certain amount of impunity. On these rare occasions, he didn't bother to speak to her, he just stared, admired, and praised her singing in a loud voice as if he'd invented her.

"We got one more set, Shorty, that's all we got to get through and then we're gone," she said. Her big black horn-rimmed glasses were fogging up in the overheated room, so she headed for the side door. Her long brown hair was hot on her neck; had she been alone, she would have twisted it into a bun and secured it with a swizzle stick.

"Until next week," he reminded her, following her outside where she could finish her cigarette in the cooler air and de-fog her glasses. "That guy with him is perfectly dressed. You don't see that very often," he added when they were outside.

"Is he your type?" she asked, half seriously. Shorty was between men, and Hackenbush knew he was happier when he was dating someone steadily.

"His clothes maybe, but did you see what a hard face he has?" Shorty asked, and went on at her nod. "He makes Mr. BJX look like a kid."

Hackenbush blew out a lungful of smoke and picked a shred of tobacco off her tongue in agreement. Bob Jones X was an overgrown kid, a vicious overgrown kid with some power now, but less anger, which made him scary and to be avoided. But the guy with him was something else, cold as ice and the hardest, deadest black eyes she'd had ever seen. Were these, she wondered, the much vaunted killer's eyes the detective novels she read went on and on about? Whatever they were, they were definitely the kind of eyes a girl in Los Angeles learned to steer clear of very quickly. No matter how weird Hackenbush's life got, it never sank to the level where human life meant nothing. BJX and his guest were gone when they went back inside.

Then it was time for the last set, which went by quickly and they were all paid in full and in their own homes by 1:30 AM, which was early for them.

One of the nice things for Hackenbush about working nights was that she could swan around town having lunch with her friends still working days. On that particular Tuesday, she would be dragging Anna Kodaly out to lunch because Anna's usual idea of lunch was tortilla chips at her desk, with salsa if she felt she needed some vegetables in her diet.

Hackenbush wasn't a model of nutrition, but most days she did better than tortilla chips for lunch. On the other hand, she smoked about a pack of unfiltered Pall Mall Reds a day, so whatever food benefit she got was wiped out right there. Well, at least she didn't do drugs...

After seeing Bob Jones X last night and working so close to Macarthur Park, drugs were on her mind. Driving home, down Wilshire through the park, she'd noticed a lot of activity in the shadows around her. Once again she swore to find another way home, but from the Coral Cave, or anywhere between Macarthur Park and Mid Wilshire, the drive home to Lincoln Heights would be much more convoluted, and probably as dangerous as the way she was doing it. That year she was driving a 1971 Volkswagon Fastback, which was almost as cute as a Karmann Ghia, but as unreliable as any old VW. What if she broke down on the way home in the wee small hours? Working pay phones were scarce in the neighborhoods Hackenbush traveled and Triple A took its time getting to tows in those parts of town.

She shoved these thoughts aside as she drove the reverse route, down Alvarado to Wilshire and then west to Temporary Insanity. The second floor offices had started out as anonymous as any office space in the east end of Westlake: bland, boring and beige. However, every artist Hackenbush knew had temped for Anna at one time or another, many had borrowed money from her, and all of them had benefited from the blond entrepreneur's down to earth good sense and business savvy. These painters, printmakers, sculptors, weavers, potters, and whatnot were a grateful bunch, so soon Anna's offices went from boring to Bohemian, bordering on opium den décor. Anna took home most of the swag she was given and, properly displayed in her Glendale bungalow, it was somewhat tamed. She kept much of the best, though conservative, work in her office, carefully spaced for maximum presentation effect. One of Linda Lim's bronze figures, an old man holding a cat, had a shelf to itself in the tiny conference room. Visitors could fish Temporary Insanity cards out of clay pot that looked like azure lace on the reception desk or get one of Anna's cards from a hand-blown glass tray on her desk. The walls had abstract oils with powerful forms, but muted colors: the kind of art that was easy for visitors to ignore, but solace and inspiration for the eyes that lived with it. Hackenbush spent a lot of time looking at these when she was there. In the reception area, there were cheerful watercolors of goldfish and flowers. Beyond thinking they were pretty, Hackenbush barely registered these paintings anymore. They were in excellent taste—everything in Anna's sphere of influence was in superb taste—and eye-catching, but they were, in Hackenbush's opinion, demanding to be admired. The other art, the art on Anna's walls at home and in her office, was there demanding to be acknowledged, if not completely understood.

Hackenbush rolled in a few minutes before noon and said hi to a girl she didn't know sitting at the reception desk. "I'm Mabel Hackenbush, I'm here–"

"Dr. Hackenbush, right? I'm Dina Lee–"

"Like the song?"

"What song?" Dina asked.

"A very old song by Eddie Cantor," Hackenbush said, wishing she'd kept her trap shut. "A nice song about a girl he loves and what he'd do for Dina Lee." Now that she was thinking about it, it was a pretty dumb song, one of many based on a girl's name where the performance rose above the material. "Are you a musician, Dina, or artist, or what?"

"I'm a dancer," Dina said, standing up to show off her dancer figure. "I met Lola Rae and Suzie Reed at a ballet workshop up in Hollywood, and they recommended me to Anna. She's wonderful. Anna, I mean, she has me working here so I can learn Lotus 1-2-3 and go out on jobs."

Hackenbush, who didn't have a dancer figure, slouched into her curves and agreed that Anna was, indeed, wonderful. "Suzie Reed's one of the coolest people in LA and an incredible dancer. Lola's got some talent, but she's insane; did you notice that?"

"How funny, that's what Lola said about you!" Dina exclaimed, clapping her hands together in a way so stagy, Hackenbush wondered if she did mime, too. "I asked her what kind of doctor you are and she said she'd tell me later, but I haven't seen her. Can I ask you? Are you really a doctor?"

"Nah, when I was five or six, I saw 'Day at the Races' and Groucho played a veterinarian, Dr. Hugo Z. Hackenbush, in it and I said I wanted to be a vet so my name would be Dr. Hackenbush, too. The Doc nickname just stuck from then on. It makes a nice name for the band, though." Hackenbush had told this story so many times she was seriously considering having cards printed up.

"But you never became a vet?" Dina asked; possibly she'd lost track of the explanation.

"Nope, I don't even like animals that much." Hackenbush winked at Anna, who'd stuck her head out of her office and waved.

Dina had another question: "Who's Groucho?"

Hackenbush's jaw hit the floor. "Who's Grou-?"

"Ha! There you are, Mabel, come on in!" Anna rushed up to save Dina from whatever Groucho lesson she was about to get. "Ross is here, with Tim Jackson, a new Insane Temp. Come meet him." She swiveled around and hissed, "Go. To. Lunch!" at Dina, who grabbed her purse and split.

"How can she not know who Groucho Marx is?" Hackenbush after the dancer was out the door.

"She's very young, Mabel," Anna said, patting her sprayed-into-submission blond hairdo. Not that there was ever a hair out of place, so those pats were more of a prim shrug by a woman raised not to shrug. "Were you born knowing about the Marx Brothers?"

"No, but that was corrected before I could walk," Hackenbush said. "Wanna hear me sing 'Whatever it is, I'm against it'? I don't remember learning that song, I've just always known it. I think my father sang me to sleep with it when I was a baby."

"He would, wouldn't he? Wanna hear a Hungarian lullaby my mother sang to me in the cradle? Same thing, Mabel, different culture," Anna said, ushering her into her office.

Yes, there was Ross, taking up most the space in Anna's office, and with him a trim young black guy wearing a suit and tie Hackenbush thoroughly approved of. He looked quite nice; even the yellow backpack slung jauntily over his shoulder added to the overall pleasing effect of his ensemble. After Anna introduced him to Hackenbush, he said Ross helped him pick the tie and the suit.

"Ross has great taste," Hackenbush said. "You should see him all dressed up."

"I have, he was at my wedding."

"Oh yeah?" She looked at Ross and then back at Tim. "How do you know each other?"

"Ross was my Big Brother when I was in high school," Tim said with a weird combination of pride and embarrassment Hackenbush thought was charming. "And he testified at my trial. Got some time knocked off, too."

"Trial?" she asked in the rather awkward silence that followed.

"Grand theft auto, drunk driving, and property damage," Ross finally said. "Well, Mabel, you see Tim here grabbed a car with some friends, got drunk and ran it into the river. Nobody got killed, but he was driving and had just turned eighteen so they threw the book at him. We got him the best lawyer we could, and he got probation and community service, but no jail time."

"Thank God," Anna said softly, gazing at Tim.

Hackenbush agreed; Tim was way too pretty for the big house. "Who's we?" she asked Ross.

"Me, Legal Aid, some of his High School teachers, and the Big Brother organization," Ross said. "I'm grateful to Anna for giving him a chance."

"Ross," Anna said in her businesswoman voice, "he has an Associate's degree in accounting from LA City College. Anyone would hire him. I'm just glad I got him." She smiled at Tim. "And you're perfect for the Monroe Company job that starts tomorrow. You're really helping me out, you know."

"I salute you, Tim," Hackenbush said. "I couldn't do accounting to save my life." This was only partly true; she could do accounting, but hated it to death.

Tim said he hoped he'd do a good job. Ross said something about being hungry and they went off to lunch.

"Would anyone hire him?" Hackenbush asked when they were gone.

"No, not even if he had angel wings and a halo,"

Anna said, sounding angry. "A young black man with a felony conviction almost doesn't have a chance to be good in this damn town."

"There's always you, Anna," Hackenbush said, leaning on her desk, hoping they were going to lunch soon. "You've helped a lot of us."

Anna looked up at her with a grim smile. "This is a two and a half week temp job for him, Mabel," she said. "It's the first job in what he studied. I'll... I'll get him a couple of more, so he has a few things on his résumé, and then I'll try to find him a perm job with some big company... He's got a pretty wife and three year old daughter, he showed me their picture..." There were tears in Anna's voice, but her eyes were dry.

Lunch could wait, Hackenbush leaned over and answered a ringing phone, took a message for Dina Lee, and hung up. "Anna, when you think Tim is ready for a perm job, let me know, I'll call everybody I know to help you find one for him." She gave Anna a reassuring smile. "He's an insane temp now, he's part of this crazy extended family you keep going."

"I'm only doing it for the kicks, Mabel," Anna said matter-of-factly.

It was hard to tell when Anna was being sarcastic, so the best course was to assume she was serious. "What kicks?" Hackenbush asked. "You scrape by every month like the rest of us and you put up with more bullshi–"

"Well, it's never dull."

"And Dina Lee! How can that child not know–"

"Mabel, please, I'm not even sure she knows who Nixon is."

This brought Hackenbush up short. "Was it that long ago?" Anna nodded. "Oh well. Does she know who Ronald fucking Reagan is?"

"I think she's heard of him, yes." Anna leaned down to open her deep desk drawer.

"Aren't you hungry, Anna?" Hackenbush asked. "Let's go find–"

"I have salsa for the chips, Mabel, I also made that onion dip you like so much," Anna said, laying out their lunch. "I have to be here for the phones. Sorry."

"Oh well," Hackenbush said, accepting a paper plate of chips and adding a dollop of onion dip à la Kodaly. "I really like this dip."

"How's it going at the Lotus Room?" Anna asked.

"Musically and food-wise very well," Hackenbush said around a mouthful of chips. "I think they'll give us five nights in the bar and Sunday brunch in the hotel restaurant next month or the month after, when the tourist season picks up."

"Can you live on that?" Anna asked, seeing, with her usual mixed emotions, one of her best temps succeeding away from Temporary Insanity.

"Yeah. Can't save much, but I can live on it if my luck holds and the car keeps running," Hackenbush said with a smile.

Anna smiled back. "They'll miss you at the Gas Company next time they ask for you."

"Tell them to come to the club to see me."

Hackenbush loved the Lotus Room, mainly because Wang the bartender made her feel not just like the only woman on earth, but the only woman on earth who could appreciate his brilliant Ramos Gin Fizzes. He was one of the few bartenders in town willing to make a brunch drink in the middle of the night. He was also the only man Hackenbush ever knew who could instinctively gauge the exact amount of gin to put in her drinks based on some mysterious intuition he had about her. Or something; Hackenbush had no idea how he knew what her gin level should be, he just knew, and that made her ridiculously happy.

Wang was a great guy. He'd heard the band at the Hotel van Gogh-Gogh and then convinced Mr. Tanaka to hire them so he'd have some decent music four nights a week. He'd originally lobbied Tanaka for five nights, but Sunday through Tuesday nights were slow that time of year. Tanaka was cautious, too; he wanted to see if a jazz combo and dance team could develop a following at the Lotus Room. Wang's enthusiasm was one thing, paying customers were another.

So far so good, though. There was a steady crowd for *Dr. Hackenbush and her Orchestra* and most nights at least half of the Storm Hill restaurant's dinner crowd, being within tasteful earshot, was lured into the bar by the music. And they stayed in the bar, drinking, for the music and the dancing. This was a very good sign for Tanaka; he even spent a little on advertising, and told the kitchen to give the band and Shorty better food. Dinner was part of the deal; someday he'd have to pay them more and also give them decent dinners. He'd cross that bridge when he came to it; for now, the band and Shorty got great food and okay wages. That they were prompt, professional, easy on the eyes, and a delight for the ears was expected, and therefore taken for granted.

Hackenbush was just glad to have four steady nights at decent pay, where Shorty got paid to dance with her. They'd always been a good dance team, but the security of regular performances was turning them into a great dance team.

The band never had a bad night at the Lotus Room. They had competent and professional nights, and those were about as bad as it got. Under Wang's watchful eye and educated ear, the quartet strove for more than just a good performance, they strove for an enlightened performance. They took risks, more and daring risks when the room was light on audience, or was full of musicians. Because they played on Wednesdays, and many of their fellow musicians had that night off, sometimes the room was full of cats. When that happened the band really took off.

These nights were a special heaven for Wang because he really loved jazz and all the creativity that went into it. The jagged edges, the walls of sound, the familiar melodies turned inside out, rising above the original and into the moment, no words could describe. For Wang, and guys like Wang, *Dr. Hackenbush and her Orchestra* were almost a philosophy. The band had versions of tunes that everyone was comfortable with, that for Wang were like slippers he could relax in. But, depending on the mood and circumstance, the same tune might take on a nuance, something startling, even disconcerting, as if the riff just slapped the listener. When that happened, sentences hung in midair, drinks stopped their way to lips, and anyone trying to tune the band out finally gave up, sat up straight and listened. Wang had seen a lot of bands, from the bar and from the audience, but very few of them grabbed a crowd like Hackenbush's could.

On a night when the civilians were in the majority at the Lotus Room, the band went easy for the first two sets. In the third set, they started to heat things up, but by then the crowd was mostly music lovers, and the non-music lovers were having a new experience, so everyone had a good time. In the fourth and final set, the band played as if they had nothing to lose, and by then, they really didn't; most of the crowd might not understand everything that was going on, but they were aware they were witnessing something important. They were seeing artists making art that lasted an instant and was gone forever.

The dancing was another matter. It was just fun to watch Hackenbush and Smith trip the light fantastic; they were funny, graceful and powerful all at the same time. Shorty was a great choreographer, even if he had to dumb it down for Hackenbush's rather limited terpsichorean abilities. Nevertheless, he got a lot out of her; what she lacked in technique she made up for with hard work. And in front of an audience, some extra flair kicked in, and Hackenbush looked like a better dancer than she actually was. That fire warmed Shorty as well, and together they were so in tune with each other and the dance that it was pure joy to watch.

Ross, Cody and Phil liked the dances because they were a kind of break for them. No improvisations, no shocking melodic or rhythmic Hackenbushian innovations on some innocent song to swerve around while making it sound like they knew she was going to do that all along. Sometimes they did know; sometimes they could see it coming, and then sometimes she chickened out of wherever she was heading and that was another musical train wreck to be dealt with. Not that they minded; they'd rather work with Hackenbush and her crazy ideas than play on auto pilot behind a blander singer with an equally lovely voice. But the dancing, that was different, that was nice, all they had to do was play the tunes the way Shorty asked them to. And, if there were no interesting people in the audience to look at, the dances, even from behind, were interesting for the musicians, who didn't dance (don't ask them).

So life was good for everyone at the Lotus Room in those days. On a break, Hackenbush asked if Ross heard from Tim. Ross said, once, but it was a very short call; Tim was too busy working to call him just to gossip.

"He's been there, what? A week now?" she asked.

"Hm... yeah, I think I saw you at Anna's a week ago yesterday," Ross said, humoring her. "So, I guess he's got next week, too."

"Maybe they'll hire him perm," she said idly.

"Didn't sound like that when Anna described the job," Ross said. "Sounded like they had some snarled up checkbooks and just needed those fixed up." He sipped his drink. "That neighborhood is too far from where he lives, too, and it's not so great."

"Tim? Tim? Tim! Is this that Tim kid you taught to drive, Ross?" Cody asked.

Mabel and Shorty exchanged shrugs; Ross and Cody were old friends and odd facts popped up between them now and then. Such as that they'd met in the LA County Honor Jazz Band, which was the cream of the crop of all LA County high school music programs.

"Yeah," Ross said. "Tim turned out okay, got a business degree and now he's working for Anna K." He looked at Hackenbush. "The hours on this job are weird, too."

"How so?" she asked, perusing the song list Phil had just handed her for the next set. Phil was organized like that and they all loved him for it, except when it pissed them off.

"First day, he got there at 9, like Anna asked, but no one had any work for him until 11," Ross said. "He said the maintenance guy let him in, gave him coffee and said to sit tight until somebody come in. Then, hmph, they asked him if he could work 11 to 7:30, not 9 to 5:30. Those aren't great hours, but he mostly misses traffic."

"Where is this job anyway?" she asked, handing the revised and improved song list back to Phil with a smile. He could put "Stella by Starlight" on his list until Hell froze and she still wouldn't sing it.

"In some building on Wilshire a block east of Alvarado."

Hackenbush looked Ross in the face. "What a crappy neighborhood to have to work a day job in. At least he can eat at Langers Deli."

Ross scowled and said Tim was probably taking his lunch. "Hmph. Man's got a family to support. No extra money for over-priced pastrami, Mabel."

Hackenbush might have argued that Langers pastrami was worth every penny, including the stress of getting to and from the restaurant, which was diagonally across the street from the south east corner of Macarthur Park at seventh and Alvarado. And in the late afternoon, which was as late as Hackenbush ever wanted to be in Langers, one could watch the Guardian Angels in their red berets patrolling the park, making it safe for, well, the bus stop across the street.

The next night, Friday night, for the first time ever, Ross sent a sub to the gig.

He was a young Latino named Lou Martinez that Phil seemed to know. Or at least the kid was willing to listen to Phil, to whom Hackenbush left the musical direction to when she felt too lazy to be bothered. Lou was a good listener and a quick learner. He played under and occasionally to the side of Hackenbush's vocals, supporting the band with some cool licks the singer would have approved of more if she'd heard them at least once before they were in front of the audience. Being young, he didn't have much in his bag of tricks and his playing sounded suspiciously like Ross'. Hackenbush later learned that he was one of Ross' students from Grove, and that Phil, who taught at Grove when the regular guitar teacher needed time off, knew him from the school's big band. When Hackenbush was an arranging student there, it was called the Tuesday play-down band, because they sight read the student arrangements.

It was the dancing that threw Lou for a loop. The poor guy had obviously never played for something that was choreographed. Not that Shorty's choreography was the most predictable thing in the world, but someone with more experience might not have syncopated the bridge to "Let's Face the Music and Dance" after seeing the dancers staying on the beat in the verses. Hackenbush never bothered to write out arrangements for the club gigs, so Lou really had nothing but his musical instincts go on. It was hardly his fault he was subbing for the great and wonderful (and now fully appreciated) Ross and was therefore tossed in over his head. After a maiming look from Wang and a few words from Phil, the drummer laid way way far back, and stayed on brushes during the dance numbers. Hackenbush and Shorty vowed to kiss Ross' feet next time they saw him.

On the first break, Lou apologized to the dancers. "Hey, I'm really sorry, I–"

"Lou, it's okay," Hackenbush cut him off. "You're doing a great job on the songs, just keep on keeping your head down during the dances. And the ballads," she added, cringing at the memory of a jagged tom-tom run in the middle of "All the Things You Are."

"Yes, please," Shorty said, rather sourly. He wasn't particularly charming to musicians who screwed up Hackenbush's dancing and made them both look bad. He'd not really noticed the jarring drum moments during her singing, but Shorty was usually distracted before the first dance number and more into the music after it.

They were interrupted by Wang asking, rather belatedly Hackenbush thought, to see Lou's ID. Fortunately Mr. Martinez was a few months past his twenty-first birthday.

Wang was carding a lot of the crowd that night; they all seemed to be friends of Lou, including one Gregg Miller who eased alongside Hackenbush, introduced himself and offered to light the singer's cigarette. "Thanks," she said coldly, filing his name away so she could forget it later.

"I really liked what you did with 'Wave' up there," he said, trying to smolder and look cool at the same time, which is a mistake Hackenbush noticed the younger set made a lot.

"Thanks." She gave him the once-over from his shaggy brown hair, threadbare sports coat, black jeans, down to his scuffed-up sneakers, and then looking off in to the middle distance as if he didn't exist.

"Some of these old songs," he bravely continued. "They have such trite melodies a good voice is all they need to sound, y'know, good."

She looked hard at him. "And phrasing?" He nodded. "And intonation?" He nodded. "And singing with the band instead of over it?" He nodded. "And not falling on my a–"

"What about the dancing?" Shorty cut her off before she could verbally decapitate the cute young guy. Gregg was more Shorty's type; skinny and in need of nurturing, fashion and otherwise.

"Uh, it was good," Gregg said, starting to look really nervous. It was dawning on him that the babe wanted to kill him and this guy wanted to–

"Just 'good'?" Shorty asked coldly.

Now they both wanted to kill him.

Phil rescued him. "Hey, Gregg, glad y'could make it," he said, tossing a fatherly arm around the kid's narrow shoulders and bravely placing his own body between Gregg and the dancers. "Wha'd'ya think of my solo on 'Wave'?"

"I liked it," Gregg said, his relief embarrassingly visible. "I thought you could have, y'know, played more of the upper chord structure–"

"That's how y'play it, Gregg," Phil said, gently. "Someday you'll get ta see it the way me 'n Hackenbush do: less is more."

Hackenbush actually thought Phil's solos were a little on the thin side on Latin tunes, but she wasn't about to agree with Gregg. "Figures he's a guitar player," she said in an undertone to Shorty. Hackenbush didn't have a lot of love for guitarists on the make. The band's previous guitar player, Eddy Lee, had eventually won and then broken Hackenbush's heart and nearly broken up the band when he jilted her and left town without finding his own replacement. Romantics will understand that a man running away from the love of his life isn't likely to tie up all the loose ends on his way out, but he let a lot of people down, and those people had long memories.

"That doesn't make him any less cute," Shorty

undertoned back at her.

"Look at his clothes, Shorty," she whispered, hoping to poison his mind against Gregg, via his sartorial sensibilities, before it all ended in tears.

"It's not the clothes, Mabel, it's the man in them," he whispered back.

She covered her laugh with a cough. "So how do you two guitarists know each other?" she asked Phil.

"I've been subbing at Grove for Joey Bell," Phil said, knocking back half a vodka tonic. He'd switch to straight 7-Up on the next break and finish the night on it. "Someday Gregg is gonna be the guitar player in town everyone wants ta sound like." He winked at Gregg. "Provided he survives meeting you, Mabel."

She laughed and accepted a Ramos Gin Fizz from Wang in a quart-size glass. "What's up with Ross?" she asked after the first heavenly sip.

"I don't know," Phil said, wrinkling his brow, which went farther and father up his scalp every year. He'd once tried a comb-over but Hackenbush couldn't keep a straight face and Ross, who was completely bald, took him aside and told him to just accept God's will for his hair. "I ran into him at Grove and he asked me ta get a sub for tonight or do without. Something had him worried. He didn't stop t'talk about it."

It was time to get back to work, so Hackenbush sucked down half her drink and asked Wang to put it in the fridge for the next break.

The next set went considerably better and she even threw in a few more vocal trills and thrills to impress Gregg Miller. Then she tried to stop because she realized the last thing she wanted to do was impress him. But, and this was a tough one, if Hackenbush knew she had one enlightened listener in the audience, she couldn't help but pull out all the stops. She noticed Phil was playing more of the upper chord structures and harmonics to impress that damn kid, too. At one point Cody leaned forward and asked them if they were auditioning for some avant-garde opera because he hoped they got that job, since they were losing most of their audience. They cooled it, but they'd made their point. Lou was in the groove on the songs and out of the way during the dances. On the whole, the second set was more of a success than the first.

"Have you talked to Ross, Cody?" she asked, stirring the second half of her enormous Gin Fizz.

"Nope."

Hackenbush drank her drink and watched the after dinner crowd roll in. Wang leaned over the bar and said something about the "younger set" taking up tables to drink soda all night. Hackenbush said something about this being an extremely unusual evening. Wang said he hoped so.

Lou overheard most of this and strolled over to say something to his fellow music students. They all migrated to the bar. And Wang was so happy, he broke out extra rations of pretzels.

Mr. Tanaka rolled in early in the third set and, eyeing the two distinct classes, if not species, of bar patron in the Lotus Room that night, frowned at the bar and smiled at the rest of the room. He took up residence at the extreme end of the bar where he could watch the room, but not the band.

He could, however, hear them, so Hackenbush and the band toned it down even more. They didn't like being wallpaper, but Tanaka paid them well enough that they didn't mind being wallpaper now and then. Only Wang expected brilliance on a regular basis, provided his boss wasn't around. This was where Gregg's unappreciated remark about the beauty of Hackenbush's voice paid off; she could sing these Tin Pan Alley tunes straight and the quality of her voice and sensibility of her subtle phrasing made the performance seem more sublime than it was. They might be wallpaper, but by God they were top-notch quality wallpaper. Which is what Mr. Tanaka wanted for the after dinner crowd; he was as worried about their digestion as he was about their wallets.

Hackenbush could see the kids at the bar wondering if, someday, they'd have a deluxe gig in a nice room like this and have to bank their fires, rein in their genius and be, y'know, boring. "Yes, children," Hackenbush thought. "Someday even you might have to cool it to keep your club boss happy. And you, too, will survive. Hey, kiddies, it sure beats the hell out of typing and filing eight hours a day."

By the fourth set, Mr. Tanaka had satisfied himself that he still had a jazz room, but a civilized one. The Grove kiddies took off unobtrusively during the break and a few solitary jet-lagged business men took their places at the bar. The dinner crowd finished up their third drink; surprised they'd ordered a third drink, the music was so good, they'd lost track of the time and they must come back very soon for more.

The room was peaceful. Shorty and Hackenbush glided around it, oblivious to everything but the music and each other, but still missing Ross because Lou, in the half deserted room, was inserting riffs where no riffs should ever be. But, oh well, Ross would be back very soon, they hoped.

And then they realized Ross was sitting at a tiny table in a very dark corner and they had no idea how long he'd been there. They finished the dance;

Hackenbush went back to the band to sing the last eight and finish the night, Shorty went to sit with Ross in the dark.

While Lou was packing up, Hackenbush, Phil and Cody joined Ross and Shorty in the dark. Shorty looked pale, even for Shorty.

"Hey, Ross, what's–" Hackenbush began.

"Tim Jackson's been murdered," Ross said, accepting a glass of scotch from Wang. "Can you keep these coming, Wang?"

"Sure, Ross." Wang had never seen Ross drink straight liquor before. None of them had. The look on Ross' face must have been enough for Wang's bartender sixth sense; he pulled the pourer out of the neck of a bottle of Cutty Sark and brought it to the table.

"They found his body in Macarthur Park early this morning, or yesterday morning, Friday morning," Ross said, drinking steadily. "I just finished up with his family." He looked at the shocked faces around him and said into the silence, "Mabel, you better call Anna Kodaly. The cops found her card on his body and called her to identify him."

Without a word, Hackenbush went to the payphones by the Ladies' room.

"Anna said his head was so bashed up, she wasn't sure it was him," he said when she was gone. "But Tim's wife, Alice, had called her office looking for him, so she had her come do the official ID. Alice asked me to come get her to go to the morgue."

"Shit." Cody leaned back in his chair. "How is she?"

"She's very messed up, will be for a long time." Ross poured more scotch in his glass.

Lou, sensing the vibe, tapped Phil on the

shoulder and said something in his ear. They went to talk to Wang, who paid Lou out of the cash register and sent him on his way. Hackenbush walked up and asked for a drink, was informed it was too late for her to drink and got a glass of cranberry juice over ice.

"Wha'd Anna say?" Phil asked, looking tired.

"She didn't pick up when I left a message, so I don't know," Hackenbush said, also tired. "I'll try again tomorrow."

"Is Ross going to be able to get home?" Wang, ever thoughtful, asked.

Hackenbush looked at Phil, and knew he had a wife to get home to, and then looked at Cody, and knew there was a girlfriend waiting for him at his place, and knew it was up to her or Shorty.

While Cody and Phil were packing up, she made her pitch. "So, Ross, uh, let's go to my place," she said lamely. "I can sleep on the couch," she added quickly.

Ross looked at her like she'd just landed from Mars. "Hmph, thanks, Mabel, but Shorty offered to drive me home."

"Where I can sleep on the couch," Shorty put in briskly.

"Oh, never a doubt, Shorty, never a doubt," Hackenbush murmured. She watched them leave, Ross steadying himself on the smaller man's shoulder. More than once Hackenbush had steadied herself on that same shoulder so she knew how strong it was. She hoped Ross would be okay, or okay enough to make the gig that night, Saturday, which sounded cold, but if he could make the gig, then Hackenbush would know he was mostly okay. Ross managed his feelings extremely well; there were some very complex, but organized emotions in that man. She'd seen him hurt and keep going. So, she predicted he'd hurt for Tim Jackson, but keep going for the good of Tim's wife and kid, the band, and maybe Anna, too.

Poor Anna... Hackenbush had never seen a dead body; she cringed a little thinking about it.

"You okay?"

She jumped finding Wang beside her, holding her coat and her ukulele case.

"Yeah, thanks. Hey, Wang, put whatever Ross drank on my tab."

"Tab schmab, Hackenbush," Wang said. "See you, and hopefully Ross, too, tonight."

"Yeah." She took her stuff and went home.

Shorty drove Ross home and then sacked out on Ross' couch. It wasn't the first time; Shorty was periodically broke and homeless and, when he wasn't in the mood for Hackenbush's cheerful irony, he stayed with Ross. He couldn't stay with Phil, who was married and uptight, and Cody's girlfriend made it clear she didn't like him, so it was good that Ross gave him a key and Shorty respected the ground rules: clean up after himself and don't bring anyone home. Ever. This last was kind of a non-issue; if Shorty was homeless and broke, it was because he was between men. At the moment he was in the early stages of a new romance and, thanks to the Lotus Room and other gigs, was solvent. So, although he had his own home to go to, he thought he'd better stick close to Ross.

He'd never seen Ross like this. Ross was a grown man, so he'd had his share of sorrow, but he never let it get him down.

"Not easy being a Black man, Shorty," he'd said in the car. "Hmph, hard to find something Negroes and Whites will let you do. Music is one thing, sports another; everything else is bein' a thug or actin' white. Me 'n Cody an' a few other guys got lucky with music. I thought Tim was gonna be okay... ah... I really did..." He dropped off from scotch, sorrow and exhaustion. Shorty woke him up just enough to get him in the house and into bed. Ever thoughtful, Shorty took Ross' shoes off before he crashed on the couch.

Ross woke the next morning and smelled the coffee. This was significant because he lived alone, but not actually interesting enough to actually wake completely up for. Then the day before crashed over him and he figured he'd better be up and around instead of lying in bed where there was nothing else to think about. He found Shorty in the kitchen unpacking eggs and a canned ham from a grocery bag.

"I went shopping on last night's tip jar," the dancer cheerfully informed him.

"I can cover that, Shorty," Ross said, accepting a cup of really good coffee, and wondering why it only tasted this way when Shorty made it.

"You can cover half. I plan to eat, too."

And eat they did. Between the two of them, they ate their way through nine eggs, a dozen pancakes, with apricot jam, butter, and maple syrup, a rasher of bacon, a mound of fried potatoes, wheat toast, and a slab of ham each.

Ross sat back with a satisfied grunt and found Shorty watching him. The dancer looked away when Ross made eye contact. "I'm okay, Shorty," he said. "Thanks."

"I'm sorry about your friend, Ross." Shorty kept looking at the middle distance, somewhere near the stove.

"Yeah. I thought he was gonna be okay," Ross said, gathering up plates. "Goddamn drugs, and the fucking idiots doing them."

"Drugs?"

"Why else would he go into that park in the middle of the night?" Ross asked rhetorically, and started washing up.

Shorty didn't say anything; in his circle Macarthur Park was too rough even for rough trade. Not that Shorty knew anything about that, but that was the received wisdom of homosexual milieu of LA in those days. Now, Griffith Park was a whole other matter.

"Thanks for breakfast, Shorty," Ross said when he dropped him at the New Watanabe so Shorty could pick up his Moped scooter.

"Oh, you're welcome, Ross," he said. "I don't have a real kitchen at my place, so it's nice to cook in one sometimes... kind of..." Shorty trailed off and glanced at the drummer.

"I'm okay, Shorty," Ross said, with a sigh, wondering how many times he'd get to say that over the next few days. "Although if anything bad ever does happens to me, you call Anna Kodaly. I'm tellin' ya now, that woman's as steady as a rock in a hurricane. I'll see you tonight."

Shorty smiled his half smile, half frown at him and got out of the car.

"It was a shock," Anna had said when Hackenbush finally got her on the phone that afternoon. She was too busy to talk, said she was fine, shocked, but fine, and she'd call Hackenbush later.

"Shocked," thought Hackenbush. "Anna is shocked. Ross is devastated. And I'm... what?"

Not involved, she decided. Tim seemed like a nice guy, but he wasn't a friend of hers. She had enough friends and they were plenty of trouble, thank you very much. She did wish she could have gone over and helped Anna somehow, like make her coffee or vacuum her house or something. Anna was shocked. Hackenbush had never seen her that way, and, although she said she was shocked, Anna's voice betrayed nothing. She might as well have said her great Aunt Zsa-Zsa was shocked by the price of goulash.

"Oh, fuck," she said, picking up her baritone ukulele, tuning it and strumming a few chords. She felt like she was letting some idea of friendship down. Hell, Shorty had slept on Ross' couch and cooked him breakfast, for Christ's sake. At least she could drive up to middle Glendale and cook Anna a... well, no, she couldn't cook very well... But she could drive up to middle Glendale and get Anna some take-out, yeah, a cheese sandwich or something.

But Anna didn't want company. And Hackenbush figured Anna was a grown woman and knew how to ask for help if she needed it. The end. On the other hand, Ross didn't ask Shorty to make him breakfast, but he must have been glad to get it. No, Anna was different, but Hackenbush would check anyway. She picked up the phone and called, got Anna's machine and left a message. Busy woman, that Anna Kodaly.

"Fine," she told herself. "I tried."

Hackenbush was a busy woman herself. That Saturday afternoon she cleaned the kitchen of her rented house in Lincoln Heights. It had been a wreck when she moved in, but a coat of paint had done wonders. She'd even rented a floor sander and re-varnished the hardwood floors. Based on that experience, she now understood why hardwood floor guys made so much money; it was a terrible job. But worth it: when they were clean those floors shone like honey in sunlight. This cheered Hackenbush, occasionally it worried her that such an obsessively domestic thing could cheer her, but she figured if she had to have kinks, getting off on cleanliness wasn't a bad one.

Another kink, almost a mandatory one, was keeping her finances in meticulous order. After scrubbing the kitchen, she sat down with her checkbook and most recent bank statement to reconcile her checkbook. Then she compared all her ATM receipts for the period against the bank statement and stapled them to it in chronological order. Her bank, First Interstate, either didn't make mistakes or caught them right away, but she kept a close eye on them anyway. Occasionally there was a phantom forty dollar ATM withdrawal that was debited (as they say in the mirror world of banking) back to zero itself out the same day. As far as Hackenbush could tell, banking and technology seemed to be getting along pretty well. There was a paper trail for every transaction and, because she kept tabs on it, this gave her sense of security—or at least relief that this was one thing in her life she could count on being right most of the time. Her own bank reconciliation was almost a game to her and, when she got all the numbers to line up, it was like figuring out a puzzle. She was terrible with puzzles, crossword puzzles made her frown and grind her teeth, but reconciling her bank account felt enough like puzzle-solving to make her feel cleverer than she was. Hackenbush frankly hated accounting jobs and finally flatly refused to do them; other people's money gave her the heebie-jeebies.

The kitchen floor had long since dried while

she was minding her meager funds. She went in to make another cup of coffee. Someday she might be in the money enough to not have to stretch the good mocha java coffee with Luckys' generic coffee. At least she was in the money enough those days be able to afford good mocha java coffee at all.

Did Tim drink coffee? "Whoa, where did that come from?" she asked out loud, trying to slam the brakes on wherever it was leading. Too late: "Did Tim drink coffee?" led to "What were his wife and kid going to do without him?" Since this was unanswerable, she moved on to "How do people survive?" She had her own problems and was barely making it, but at least she was scraping by in her art, and not in someone's fucked up office. An even bigger question for Hackenbush was "How do people with kids survive?" She'd known her share of welfare mothers; none of her acquaintance ever thrived and usually they drifted away because the daily demands of survival on five hundred or so dollars a month and food stamps precluded time for friendship with fascinating creatures like Hackenbush. The only one she was still in touch with was heading into her third self- and kid-supporting year at the piano bar at a swanky Westside hotel, so she wasn't even a welfare mother anymore. She'd gone through the Grove piano performance program on AFDC, a Pell Grant, a Cal Grant, one twenty-five hundred Student Loan, and a thousand from Jewish Free Loan, which were no interest student loans requiring only two co-signers. Hackenbush had had one of those herself for fifteen hundred to pay her Grove tuition, long ago. Her father's friends Aunt Marie and Uncle Phil had co-signed for her, because she was too proud to ask Louis Hackenbush for anything in those days. Marie and Phil also had better credit than Big Daddy Hackenbush, in case anyone was checking on such things.

The next and penultimate unanswerable question in this sequence was: "How do people have the courage to have children in this fucked-up world?" And the last question was "Who the fuck knows?"

So many unanswered questions had her ornery and in the mood to butt against something. In honor of all this, she put on Charles Ives' "The Unanswered Question" and made it through eight whole minutes before she was ready to resume normal life and listen to Billie Holliday from the thirties. She sang along while she swept her glowing amber-colored floors.

Anna rambled around her house for as long as she could stand it and then fled to the grocery store. She lost herself in the local Albertsons buying labor-intensive comfort food: ingredients for meatloaf, chicken soup with dumplings, stuffed peppers, gingerbread, and rice pudding. Shopping helped, but she still couldn't stop thinking about the day before.

She'd never seen a dead body at the morgue and hoped she'd never see another one. Officer Casey called around three that afternoon because they found one of her cards on the body of a young black male in the park and it was all they had to go on. Not that the police told Anna this, but they'd found the body at dawn. It was a busy day at the morgue and Rampart police department so nobody got around to doing anything about contacting her until mid-afternoon.

Back at her little house, Anna unloaded her groceries and washed some vegetables for a salad. She thought perhaps she should have invited Hackenbush over for lunch or dinner, but even thinking about spending time with another human, even one as understanding—in her fashion—as Hackenbush was exhausting. Anna knew that Hackenbush worried about her and her finances, but had Hackenbush thought about it a little more or had a less romantic vision of Anna Kodaly and Temporary Insanity, she'd have realized that Anna was doing well enough to afford her mortgage, insurance and everything else that went with home ownership. It was that home ownership was such an exotic idea, Hackenbush could never get her mind around it and thought it was something to worry about.

Not that Anna was rolling in dough; far from it. She was able to save very little and prospering in business sometimes meant tiding a good temp over with a small loan or nursing one back to health. She felt that just came with the territory. And it was a two-way street; Hackenbush, Linda Lim, Sandy Garner, Shorty, and many others had, at one time or another, brought her chicken soup and cleaned her house when she was sick, done her grocery shopping, driven her to the doctor, minded the office for minimum wage (when she could force them to take it) or free (usually), gone on crappy temp jobs to impress new clients or smooth down disgruntled existing ones. Anna was raised Catholic and thought of her friends as good Christians. They thought of themselves as pragmatic altruists who, although they had no real proof that what goes around comes around, helped whoever they could whenever they could just in case it was true. Hackenbush called it Zen Judiasm; she was never the first to rush to anyone's aid, but she was often the one whose faith, hard work, and efficient bitchiness turned the tide, swept up the pieces, tied up the loose ends, and booted everyone in the ass to get them moving in the right direction again.

Anna would never forget the night Suzie Reed had asked Hackenbush, Ross and Anna among the more than a dozen friends there, to intervene with her friend and fellow dancer, Lola Rae. Always high strung and slightly wacky, Lola had fallen into the clutches of a drug dealer who called himself Bob Jones. According to Suzie and Hackenbush, Bob Jones was the reincarnation of a low-life street dealer around East Hollywood in 1984 who called himself Mr. X. He'd vanished for a year and then resurfaced as Bob Jones, or as Hackenbush had rechristened him: Mr. Bob Jones X, which would have been funny if, with his newfound affluence, there wasn't so much menace. He annoyed Hackenbush more than he unnerved her; she made her anger cover her fear. Nevertheless, Hackenbush had talked him out of taking Lola on a trip to sunny South America. A trip they knew the coked-out Lola would never come back from. She'd made a breezy-sounding argument that Lola would only slow him down and he'd bought it. The infuriated, nearly psychotic Lola had to be forcibly restrained from killing Hackenbush. Much later Lola realized what a favor Hackenbush had done her and sent her a Chanukah card in March. Neither of them ever spoke of Hackenbush's bravery, but, then again, they didn't talk much on those rare occasions when they couldn't avoid each other.

Anna smiled a little over what good friends she had and that they'd been able to save Lola from, well, if truth be told, to save Lola from herself. Anna didn't believe that just saying no and long jail terms were any kind of solution to drug addiction. She believed in personal responsibility and a supportive community to help addicts and other miscreants stay clean with work, education, and fellowship. People were human, they made mistakes and there were a lot of ways to make mistakes in this world. Did it have to be fatal?

Did it? Is that why Tim Jackson died? He made the mistake of going into the park to get drugs. That's what the police thought. That's how it looked to them. This had shocked his wife, Ross and Anna very much; Tim didn't seem...

"I only met him once," Anna said grimly to the tomato she was cutting up. "How the hell would I be able to tell?"

She'd had trouble identifying the body because the face was so messed up. The body was the general build she remembered, but she couldn't be sure. She called Dina at the office to get Tim's home phone and then called his wife, Alice, who'd called earlier in the day looking for him. Alice apologized and said he'd never stayed out all night and she was calling everyone she could think of.

After Alice called that morning, Anna called the job Tim was on, finally getting an answer around one in the afternoon, and learned he was a no-show. Well, it was the last day of the job for Tim anyway, he'd asked to be replaced on it because he felt uncomfortable there. When pressed he just said he felt weird there and didn't like the hours or the neighborhood. Anna could understand the last two—that office liked to start late in the day and the blocks around Macarthur Park were creepy. Anna knew this was true; she'd had her first office down there because it was so cheap, and with good reason, stepping around junkies and homeless crazies, the dirt, the traffic, the crime all got old very fast. But when Tim said he felt "weird," Anna had wondered at his professionalism. She knew it was his first job with her, she wished he could have explained it better.

But what she really wished was that she'd told him to grab his stuff and leave that second. Instead she'd asked him to stay one more day to finish the week so she could find a replacement. At the time it had seemed like a harmless request.

Her appetite vanished, Anna put the salad fixings in a plastic bowl and into the fridge. She sat at her kitchen table by the window and looked out at her back patio. "I asked him to stay and he agreed and then he was dead," ran through her head over and over.

When she picked up the phone at the morgue to call Alice Jackson, she had to put it down until she stopped shaking. If that was Tim's body in there, then she'd killed him. Had she? Maybe, she didn't know, but she pulled herself together and called, kept her voice steady and told Alice where she was and how to get there. Then she called Dina to pick up her messages and return calls while she waited. It was times like this she wished she had a business partner to help out. She told Dina she wouldn't be back, but would be calling in for messages every hour until six, when they closed. Dina didn't have keys, but the building manager, Mr. Hernandez, would lock up for them.

"Did I kill him?" she asked herself over and over. "To keep a client happy?"

Alice arrived with Ross and they both identified Tim's body, while Anna held Tim's daughter, Alicia. Anna and Ross filled out the morgue paperwork and said they'd let them know where to send the body. There would be an autopsy, it would take a few days, maybe a week. Ross drove Alice and little Alicia home and, at Ross' request, Anna stayed with them there. While waiting for Alice's and Tim's families to come over, she made dinner with what she could find:

meatballs with gravy and mashed potatoes. None of the adults were very hungry, but it was a big hit with Alicia. After dinner, Anna spent a lot of time cleaning the kitchen (she'd have a dry cleaning bill for her suit to prove it, too) until the families had assembled and she could leave. She was home around eleven that night and fell into bed. She woke and listened to Hackenbush's message, resisting the urge to lunge for the phone and beg the singer to come there immediately so she could confess that she'd killed Tim. She wanted Hackenbush to come over and tell her she hadn't killed him. She wanted Hackenbush to come over and chase this terrible terrible feeling away.

But Anna was an adult and she knew this was her problem to get through by herself. In the hours before dawn, she went over and over it: why was Tim in the park getting killed in the middle of the night? Why did people go into that park? Mainly for drugs. If Tim was secretly on drugs, there wasn't much Anna could do about it. Yes, she should have pulled him off the job when he asked her to, but... but how, in God's name, could she have known? How could she have known one more day would kill him?

Over dinner at the New Watanabe that night Ross asked how Lou Martinez did on drums. Mr. Tanaka, at Wang's request, fed the band their pre-gig dinner in a little dining room behind the Storm Hill restaurant's kitchen. They'd tried to eat in the bar or dining room, but they had too many fans and couldn't eat in peace. The Storm Hill had some of the best Japanese food in town, even Mr. Tanaka felt the band should be able to enjoy what he allowed them to have of it in peace.

"He was okay," Hackenbush said. She might

have dissected Lou a little more, but Phil shot her a warning look. She'd suspected the kid was one of Ross' protégées, but if he was also a friend of Phil's, she'd better leave him alone. Ross, she could argue with, but arguing with Ross and Phil at dinner before a four set gig would be stupid and could affect their playing, which might, to the untrained ear, reflect badly on her. And Ross was still looking a little fragile, even though Shorty thought he was over the worst of it. Then she decided, fuck it, they're all tough enough to work with her, they can handle it. "He's really good on the up-tempo tunes, where he can play in the pocket and make snide drummer riffs here and there, which is proof positive he's learning from you, Ross." Ross smiled at this. "He played too loud on the first half of the first ballad, but that was probably nerves and he cooled it."

"He survived a scathing Hackenbush glare, Ross," Cody said, dipping a tempura shrimp in sauce. "That kid will live forever." He neglected to say he himself had leaned over Lou and said he was too loud for the tune. That the kid could learn on the fly meant he'd live forever and a day.

"And then he was a little confused about the dance numbers," Shorty said kindly. "But by the second set, he had it figured out."

"Figured out?" Ross asked Hackenbush, knowing she wouldn't mince words.

"Figured out he and his syncopated improvised drum ideas better stay the fuck out of the way of the dancing," she said, munching a piece of kappa sushi liberally slathered in sinus-clearing wasabe and salty soy sauce. It was the best decongestant, even when she wasn't congested, she knew.

"I'm sorry, Ross," Phil apologized. "I'd meant

to go over the gig before we started but I got caught in traffic, and–"

"Is that why he was here a half hour early?" Shorty asked. "Wang was wondering."

"Oh, the poor kid," Hackenbush said in a rare moment of female compassion.

"Poor kid?" Cody asked gruffly. "When I got here, he was half way through a deluxe teriyaki dinner."

"Wang thought he was too thin, too," Shorty said.

Hackenbush laughed. Wang just wanted good music and happy, well-fed, well-hydrated people around him. And, in the final analysis, wouldn't that be a perfect world for everyone? "What did Lou say about us?" she asked.

"Not much," Ross said, cutting up a huge grilled prawn that made Hackenbush wish she'd ordered that. "He thanked me for sending him," Ross paused to look Hackenbush in the eye, and added, "He said he learned a lot."

"Well, that's good!" Hackenbush clasped her hands in front of her cleavage. "I doubt he'll ever leave you in the dust, Ross, but he might make a mighty fine drummer one day. What does he want to do in music?" she asked.

"Hm, whatever passes for rock 'n roll these days," Ross said, finishing his dinner.

"A waste, but, oh well," Hackenbush said, wiping her mouth and applying lipstick.

A waiter stuck his head in and asked if he could clear the table. They said yes, and went into the bar and to work. It was a very busy Saturday night at the Lotus room, lots of tourists and civilians for the first two sets, and a serious jazz crowd for the last two, which meant *Dr. Hackenbush and her Orchestra* had to live up to and maybe a little beyond their reputation late that night. They were up to it, but it also meant they talked music on breaks, so Hackenbush never did get to ask Ross how he was. He was into the music, demanding a lot from her and the band, and Hackenbush figured if his head was in the music, he was okay.

They were back at the Coral Cave that Monday. Hackenbush liked everything about the gig but the money and the crowd. The dinner was excellent and if there was leftover food at the end of the night, the chef made care packages for the band to take home. He said he worried they didn't eat right. Cody thought this was because they fell on the food he served them, not because they were starving—although sometimes it was their main meal of the day—but because the food was incredibly good. Perfectly grilled steaks, garlicy mashed potatoes, stir fried vegetables, broiled fish in tangy sauces, and even tofu dishes the carnivores like Hackenbush, Ross and Phil scarfed up. The food made the less-than-fabulous money more palatable. So far the band hadn't had to turn down any better-paying jobs on a Monday night, but Cody had already sent a sub once when he had a better gig in a Beverly Hills club. Hackenbush didn't blame him; he was working with a fine pianist named Lewis Lewis, who was filling in for another duo, and the gig was twice what Cody would have made that night at the Coral Cave. No, Hackenbush didn't blame Cody for it, and the sub he sent did a fine, if not memorable, job.

The Coral Cave also didn't have Mr. Tanaka's ban on cats sitting in. This was nice since they could invite their friends in for a share of the tip jar, which wasn't much, but was picking up lately. That night they had Lou Martinez on congas, but not during the dances, and Gregg Miller, subbing for Phil, almost impressing Hackenbush on guitar. She managed to hide how much she liked a couple of his solos by comparing them to what she thought the long-gone Eddy Lee might have done with the tune, and finding them both lacking. Yes, "Some Other Spring" deserved better than Gregg or Ed, or even Phil, who, for all his fussiness, had a deft touch on a ballad. Now, Phil actually listened to Hackenbush's phrasing and appropriated and improved on the best of it for his solo. Hackenbush then repossessed and polished those phrases from Phil into a most wondrous thing of beauty. And of course every performance was different, but it kept them all fresh. It had taken Hackenbush a while to really get into Phil's playing because it was so subtle and cool, and was more about the song than his idea of the song. She was used to guitar players like Eddy Lee who imposed their ideas on the song to the point that if the singer, Hackenbush, didn't follow along, it sounded like she was in the wrong room. She and Eddy had hashed out their musical differences and were able to rise to the best of the music. But Eddy had been gone for over two years, and Phil had become a blessing she could now appreciate. It was one of the better-known secrets among LA music-lovers that she was, in fact, a better singer since Phil joined the band. Hackenbush claimed she'd matured as an artist through her sorrow; the rest of the world knew she was a better singer because Phil would make her sound like a braying donkey if she didn't get hip.

So, Gregg was playing guitar solos and accompaniments, not as well as Phil, but Hackenbush could feel he had potential. She only hoped he'd be able to realize it someday. And then she forgot about him.

No, it wasn't the night, or the food, or the management of the Coral Cave that bothered Hackenbush, but the crowd she was attracting. No, she wasn't kidding herself: once the coke-dealing, import-export, overdressed, too loud, bon vivant with his sandy hair blow-dried to perfection Mr. Bob Jones X had found her at the Coral Cave on Monday nights, he and his creepy coked-out rolled-up hundred-dollar bill flashing crowd were all over the club. They were a jittery bunch, but big spenders; the tip jar had tripled since they started coming in and, although they never ate more than a few bites of the magnificent food they ordered, they kept the kitchen busy. She heard they were tipping the wait staff as well as they were tipping the band. The downside was there were no leftovers, so no care packages. Ah well, one could want, but never have, everything.

"Goddamn, Bob," she said to Ross on a break. She looked more nervous than pissed off.

"Mabel, he's leaving you alone," Ross said reasonably, knowing that would irritate her enough to shake her out of her funk. "Man's got a right to hear you sing, whether you like him or not."

"He gives me the creeps," she admitted, annoyed that she felt she had to admit it. Why did Ross have to be so fucking reasonable all the time? Why? Why not be irrational now and then? Just to break up the monotony.

"Ignore him," Ross said, knowing she was close to losing her temper.

"Okay!" she hissed, losing her temper and getting over her tension at the same time. "Okay. I'll ignore him." At that moment a waiter brought her a

Ramos Gin Fizz, which took her mind right off BJX. Until the waiter pointed out BJX as the person who bought her the drink. She smiled with her mouth and drank her drink. Hey, why waste it? "Goddamn Bob," she said to herself.

Ross sighed as if he heard her thought, and this made her smile.

Yeah, the room was full of the cocaine crowd, and worse, there were half a dozen guys like Bob. They were enjoying the food, the show, the scene, and being pleasant to each other. Hackenbush had never been too close to the drug scene, but in the old Mr. X days, they were constantly having turf and supply wars. People were beaten up and occasionally killed. Mr. X had borrowed some money from her and begged a ride to the Greyhound station to avoid being killed. He'd never paid her back, but she figured that was fine. She'd been so glad to see him get the fuck out of LA just then, she didn't really need that fifty bucks back. It was worth it to get rid the little pest.

But now he was back, and he looked like, wherever he went that time, he'd graduated from being a little pest to being a scary menace. Not only did he have lots of money, and flashy suits, he also had two, sometimes three, thuggish bodyguards.

The Coral Cave set-up did give her some comfort. The band was on a slightly raised stand at the back of the room, with the kitchen and the back door on the other side other wall. When Bob and his crowd started coming in, she'd checked out an escape route if bullets or barstools started flying. She'd never been in a gunfight, but she didn't want to get hit with a cocktail table either. Turns out Cody had the same idea, and they agreed best way out was through the kitchen, and rearranged the instruments on the stand to facilitate that. Ross and Phil thought they were paranoid; Hackenbush and Cody hoped they were right. Shorty just grimaced his half smile, half frown and patted Hackenbush's arm consolingly.

"Do you think I'm crazy, Shorty?" she'd asked.

"No, dearie, I don't think you're crazy," he said sweetly. "I know you're crazy."

Ross laughed and punctuated that remark with a rim shot. It was the last time an escape route was discussed, but the instruments stayed arranged on the stand for the best and fastest route into the kitchen.

So, overall, it wasn't a bad gig, not until the Monday they came in and there were tables where Hackenbush and Smith were supposed to dance.

Looking back, Cody realized that he'd only ever seen Hackenbush annoyed. Over the years, he'd mistaken that for anger, but what came over her when she saw the tables on the dance floor, which told her Shorty was fired, was utterly terrifying. Cody thanked whatever deity protects bass players that the rage was directed at the club owner, and not him or anyone he cared about.

"Why don't you all have something to eat while the doctor talks to Mr. Arroyo?" the head waiter suggested nervously. "You, too, Mr. Smith. Please. Please?"

They ordered a delicious dinner and were treated to a show of Hackenbush arguing with the club owner and both of them getting progressively more angry. At one point the foolish man stalked off into the kitchen, Hackenbush hot on his heels. Several crockery crashes and high pitched screams from the cooks later, the club owner emerged looking deeply shaken. Hackenbush strolled out a few seconds later eating a bowl of something and looking victorious.

The head cook, that lover of good food, good music and good-lookin' women like Hackenbush peeked out and got a thumbs up from the singer over whatever she was eating.

Cody thought Hackenbush might be eating some part of the club owner, like his liver or his soul, but kept that to himself. This horrible train of thought was derailed by the club owner himself, poor devil, handing Shorty an envelope and making apologetic noises and something about free dinners as long as the band was still there. He scurried away when Hackenbush, having finished whatever she was eating, wandered up to the table.

"He paid you for tonight, right?" she half asked, half sighed at Shorty.

Shorty put away the envelope of cash and said thanks. "I guess I can take a cab home," he said glumly. He'd rather dance than do anything, so getting paid only took a little of the sting out of his disappointment that he was fired.

"I'll twist some cab fare out of–" Hackenbush began, but Ross cut her off.

"Here, Shorty," he said digging out his keys and handing them to the dancer. "If you want to hang out at my place tonight, I'll give you a lift home in the morning. Or I can come by and get the car tonight or tomorrow."

Shorty said he'd like to stay at Ross' and cook since Ross had a nicer kitchen than he did. "How will you get home?" he asked, setting his knife and fork at ten o'clock on his plate, and folding his napkin.

"Hmmm... I'm sure Mabel Ferocious can give me a lift," Ross said.

"Your place isn't anywhere fucking near my way home, but I'll have lots of energy left over," she said, her voice rising to a well modulated scream. "Since there won't be any dancing tonight!"

Ross, Cody, and Shorty were suddenly very busy standing up and pulling their cuffs down and three waiters were all over the table noisily clearing it. Hackenbush remained seated and lit a cigarette in a study of unconcern, bordering on ennui. She waved at a tall man with a barrel chest and long stork legs. "Hey, Samuel!" she yelled, glad to see him.

Ross and Cody were just glad he was there to lighten her mood. Not so long ago, they'd hoped she and Samuel Lowe would hook up, but no sparks ever flew between them, even though Samuel was a decent guy, a sometimes great trombone player, and gainfully employed as a freelance private investigator because he knew he would only ever be a sometimes great trombone player. He worked for a string of insurance companies and Hackenbush had even typed up a few reports for him. It had seemed like a match made in heaven, but nothing ever came of it. Well, they were all still friends, so that was something at least.

Shorty had been lukewarm on a Hackenbush-Lowe romance; he liked Samuel, but didn't think he was tough enough to survive the white-hot creative fire that came off Hackenbush when she was growing as an artist. Samuel would want someone he could hang out with, make music with, and grow old with, not someone whose continual artistic and personal evolution would be like trying to live with an active volcano, which was, alas, often covered with ice. But since it never worked out, even Shorty was glad to see him. He winked at Hackenbush and danced a few steps on his way out.

"Hullo, Mabel," Samuel said, gallantly kissing the hand she extended. "Where're you and Shorty supposed to dance in here?"

She snatched her hand away and told him that was a very bad question. "Bring your horn?" she asked on the heels of her rudeness.

"Nah, I came to talk to Ross," Samuel said. He sat next to her and nodded at Ross, who was watching them. Then he waved at Phil, who was arriving uncharacteristically late for Phil.

Hackenbush looked at her watch. She wasn't terribly in the mood to sing, but after the prima donna absoluta fit she'd thrown on the bastard club owner, she didn't think she ought to push her luck anymore. There was the band to think of, and her own money for the evening, and if lots of cats sat in, she wouldn't have to sing very much anyway. But it was time to get started and whatever else the club was doing wrong, as least they were introducing her correctly: "And now, direct from the middle class, the fabulous Dr. Hackenbush!"

"Can you stand to hear me sing a set and talk to him on the first break?" she asked Sam, stubbing out her Pall Mall and getting up.

"Wild horses couldn't drag me out of here before at least two sets," he said, fixing his admiring baby blues on her.

"Reaaaallly, Mr. Lowe," she drawled. "Keep that up and you'll enhance my self-esteem." She headed for the band and got half way through the first set before the gunfight started.

Gunshots are a fact of life in Los Angeles, but gunshots less than a hundred yards away, accompanied by screaming, were unusual in Hackenbush's experience. The band as well; "All the Things You Are" came to an abrupt halt mid chorus. Breaking glass and a minor stampede snapped them out of it. They dropped their instruments and ran for the kitchen. Samuel grabbed the stunned Hackenbush and hustled her into the kitchen in front of him.

"Everybody down!" he yelled, and then threw himself on top of Hackenbush.

They could hear screaming and bullets hitting the back wall, and, horribly, one of Ross' cymbals. Hackenbush tried to make eye contact with the drummer, but he had his eyes clenched shut in pain. She could only pray that they weren't hearing Cody's bass or Phil's guitar being shot up. As it turned out, miraculously, they weren't.

Nobody got up until the sirens were right out front. Then they moved very slowly so as not to spook the police, who arrived too late to arrest anyone who might have been shooting up the place. Much to Hackenbush's relief, there were no dead bodies in the room, just lots of smashed up tables and glass.

"We must live under a lucky star, Sam," she said. "Looks like Ross only lost a tom-tom and a high-hat." They looked on as Cody and Phil examined their instruments, were flooded with relief that they were undamaged, and then consoled Ross for his loss.

"Of course if the cops make this a crime scene, nothing, including those instruments can be removed," Samuel mused, hoping his casual tone would keep Hackenbush calm.

She stayed fairly calm; Samuel only heard her grind her teeth and growl "Fuck!" because he was right next to her.

Samuel and one of the police officers exchanged nods, and Samuel went over to talk to him. Hackenbush figured she wasn't going to get a drink at what was left of the bar, and the club owner looked as shattered as his club. She almost felt sorry for him.

"Maybe you do live under a lucky star, babe," Samuel said, looking pleased with himself. "Since nobody got killed, the police might be willing to let the band take their stuff after they get statements."

"We didn't see anything," she said, completely forgetting to thank him for whatever he said to the cop.

"Then it won't take very long to tell them that, hon," Sam said, patiently. "Maybe we should sit down," he suggested, "you're looking a little pale." He found an intact chair and got her into it. He wished he could get her something to drink. She wasn't in shock, but she was obviously coming off an adrenalin surge and looking very spacey. Standing in the shot-up club, they all were in different stages of spacey.

Because it wasn't a murder case, or because they didn't really care about it, and because no one could really tell them anything, the cops made short work of getting statements and getting out. The officer Samuel had talked to did them a big favor and convinced his supervisor to let the band pack up and go home.

By that time, Hackenbush was back up to speed and went looking for the club owner to see about getting them paid. But the club owner had gone home and there was no cash in the register when the chef looked. "Maybe tomorrow," he said, but they both knew this was overly optimistic.

Samuel gave Ross and what was left of Ross' drum kit a ride home.

"Hmmp, well, that was pretty fucked up, wasn't it, Sam?" Ross said when they were underway.

"Yeah."

"You shoulda brought your horn."

"I will next time," Sam said.

"There will be no next time, pal," Ross said. He stared darkly at the city going by.

"I actually came to talk to you, Ross."

"Hm?"

"Anna Kodaly asked me to tell you what I found out from the police," Sam said. "She hired me to talk to them about Tim Jackson because they were stonewalling her." He waited in vain for Ross to say "Hm," and continued: "She wanted to know why they're not investigating his murder."

"Anna K is a nice white lady, but she's kind of an idiot," Ross said quietly. "Did you tell her one more dead black man in Macarthur Park means nothing to the LAPD?"

"No, I told her a detective I know at Rampart warned me to stay out of it and get Anna to shut the fuck up before something happens to her," Sam said, turning onto Ross' street. "They're not investigating your friend's murder because it's tied up with something else, something bigger–"

"Bigger, huh?" Ross asked bitterly. "Bigger than a good man, a black man, a father and a husband's life? Yeah, that sounds like fucking LA."

Samuel parked in front of Ross' house. "They want this to be just another drug killing, Ross," he said. "I told Anna to drop it. I don't think she will, she got a copy of the autops–"

Shorty knocked on the passenger window. "This is way too early, Ross. What's up?" he said when Ross rolled down the window.

"We interrupting something, Shorty?" Ross asked, getting out of the car and walking around to the trunk.

"I wish," Shorty said, taking the shot up cymbal from him. "What the...?"

"There was a shooting at the club, Shorty," Sam began.

"OH MY GOD HE KILLED HER!"

"Shhhh! This is a nice neighborhood, Shorty," Ross hissed furiously at him. He took Shorty by the arm and between he and Sam him got into Ross' house.

"Who killed who, Shorty?" Sam asked the swooning dancer when they were inside.

"The club owner," Shorty wailed quietly. "Hackenbush beat him up–"

"She did?" Sam asked Ross, who shook his head and frowned.

"Well, she got me paid–"

"Hmph, and you the only one who got paid tonight," Ross grumbled. "What's that smell?"

"Cookies. So Hackenbush is okay?" Shorty asked.

"She's fine," Sam said.

"But unpaid," Ross added. "Are there cookies in there?" He jerked his thumb at the kitchen.

"On the counter," Shorty said. "Batch two is in the oven. So what happened?" he asked Sam because Ross was on his way into the kitchen.

"A gunfight started outside and moved inside," Sam said simply. "Nobody was killed, but there was damage. What kind of cookies?"

"Enhanced chocolate chip," Shorty answered. "Are Cody and Phil okay?" he asked Sam, and also Ross who'd just joined them with a plate of cookies.

"Yeah, and only Ross' drums got damaged," Sam said, eyeing the cookies of the platter. "Shorty, what the fuck have you done to these cookies?"

"That was my question, too," Ross said.

Shorty stood a little taller to defend his cookies.

"I buy that dough in the tube, and get some M&Ms, and nuts, and sparkles and fix them up."

This seemed reasonable to Ross and Sam so they took a cookie each, while Shorty went into the kitchen to take the second batch out of the oven. "Very festive, Shorty," Ross yelled at him.

"Thanks!" he yelled back.

"Ross, I gotta go home," Sam said, suddenly feeling very tired. "Shorty, do you want a ride home? I'm heading your way."

After a brief consultation with Ross, Shorty packed up half of the cookies and the groceries he'd bought for the next day's breakfast and went home to his own place. He liked Ross' kitchen, but would rather sleep in his own bed than on Ross' couch any night. Ross could wash one cookie sheet and survive on what he'd originally had in the fridge. He didn't ask the exhausted-looking Sam any questions on the way up to East Hollywood.

Hackenbush got home and barely got her clothes off before she fell into bed. She probably would have slept until noon except for the goddam knocking on her door at ten thirty. She looked out her front window and saw a white guy in khakis and a polo shirt. "What?" she asked through the security door.

"I have a delivery for Ms. Mabel Hackenbush," the guy said nervously.

Hackenbush noticed his shirt had the words "Bonded courier" on them and figured he might be nervous in her neighborhood. "Who from?" she asked, lighting a cigarette.

The guy consulted his slip. "'Acme Import Export'," he read. "Over on the Westside."

Hackenbush shrugged and opened the door to

sign for the manila envelope. She had to produce her driver's license to be allowed to have the parcel, and the guy was as glad to leave as she was to see him go. There were several sealed envelopes inside, with lots of tape and seals before she got to the stack of twenties. Fifty twenties to be exact and an Acme Import Export card with Mr. Bob Jones X's name on it. She gently put the money on a shelf by the door and turned the card over. No note, but lots of telephone numbers on the face of it. She dialed until she got BJX on the phone. "What the fuck is this, Bob?"

"Heard there was trouble at the club last night," he said.

"Yeah."

"I heard Ross' drums got shot up."

"Yeah."

"I heard you didn't get paid."

"Yeah."

"I'm just tryin' to, y'know, help you, Hackenbush," he said.

"Why?"

"Well, I wasn't there last night..."

"Yeah."

"And I was kinda hoping, y'know, when I wasn't there..."

"Yeah."

"Nothing would happen," he said. "Hello? Are you still here?" he asked after some silence went by.

Hackenbush smoked her cigarette and thought about this. Even without her first cup of coffee, she figured out what the little weasel was saying. "Bob," she said low and deadly. "You. Are. Bad. Trouble. And I want you to stay the fuck away from me and the band and my friends."

She hung up on him and called Samuel Lowe.

"How can I tell if some money is okay?" she asked.

"Like what? Cash?"

"Yeah. From Mr. X, remember him? He's now Mr. Bob Jones X."

"Have lunch with me," he said. "I'll be there to pick you up at noon."

Hackenbush pulled herself and a cup of coffee together a little before Samuel, punctual as ever, arrived.

"Hey, beautiful, how you holding up?" he asked, giving her a peck on the cheek, and turning down a cup of coffee.

"Fine. It's there," she said, pointing to the money on the shelf.

Samuel examined the bills, marking them with a special pen, and took a close look at the wrappings. "Since he sent it with a legit courier and not a thug, I think it's okay. Not even old Mr. X would jump through this many hoops to send you dirty money."

"Everything about him is dirty," she said, finishing her coffee. "This is guilt money. He thinks the club got shot up because of him."

"Did it?"

"Probably. Now that I think of it, last night was the first night he wasn't there from the first set," she said. "That club was the only one he could see me at lately. Wang and Tanaka warned him away from the Lotus Room."

"And this is why," Sam said. He had a deep respect for Wang's insight into who he allowed into his bar. "When did you talk to Mr. Bob Jones X?"

"After I got the money. He enclosed a card," she said, showing him it.

"Oh, well, then this money is pristine and you can spend it in good health, hon," Sam said. "Mr. X is a jerk, but I don't think he's stupid enough to put his business card on dirty money. Whatcha gonna do now?"

"With the dough? Split it with the band and Shorty," she said, stuffing the money into an envelope and tucking it into her baritone ukulele case . "That Coral Cave gig is over as far as I'm concerned and we needed something to tide us over until we get another weeknight gig not on a Lotus room night. I'm hungry, let's go."

They walked around the corner to El Tepayac on North Broadway and talked mostly about music and gigs. They even delved briefly into the past.

Over some really excellent guacamole, Sam ventured, "Too bad we never hooked up, Hackenbush."

"Sam, you're the nicest guy I know," she said. "If we'd hooked up, would I still be saying that?"

"Probably not."

"You're the smartest guy I know, too." She let the smile reach her eyes, and Sam wished he was a little bolder than smart, but knew she was a hundred and ten percent right. He steered the conversation back to music and gigs.

Hackenbush forgot to ask him why he wanted to talk to Ross the night before, and when she remembered later in the afternoon, it didn't seem all that important. She figured if it was important, someone somewhere would let her know.

There was much rejoicing when she called the band and told them there was money for the previous night. She divvyed it up as a hundred and seventy-five each for herself, Cody, Phil, and Shorty and the remainder for Ross for his damaged drums. Nobody asked where the money came from, but Ross took a moment to tell her it would take more than that much to replace his tom-tom and high-hat. She said she knew, he said he knew she knew. They cut their call short when a caterer called on the other line to book the band, alas not Shorty, for a South Pasadena casual that coming Sunday.

"God well and truly provides," Hackenbush thought, calling the band back to give them the details of the Sunday casual. She forgot to ask Ross about Samuel, and was on the verge of calling him back, when Anna called and asked her if she could drop by the office for lunch the next day. Hackenbush usually went to the Laundromat on Wednesdays but figured she could work around it if she went to the Temporary Insanity before noon. This meant getting up a little earlier, but lunch with Anna, and hopefully not onion dip again, was worth it.

Shorty called and asked if she wanted to come to his place for dinner. She accepted, feeling her day was turning out better than she'd thought it would. She spent an hour playing her baritone ukulele and musing on what she wanted to do, or rather what she wanted Phil and Ross to do differently, on "Love Me or Leave Me," which was boring. Boring to sing and boring to listen to and on the verge of being removed from her song list. By the time she was ready to leave for Shorty's bachelor digs, she'd decided that she wanted Phil and Ross to stay out of "Love Me or Leave Me" until the bridge and then just play little riffs here and there until their solos and the last chorus. It wasn't that she didn't love Phil and Ross anymore, it was just they were overwhelming a song that was on the weak side to begin with. And, no, it wasn't Hackenbush's fault it was a weak song, but it was her problem. And yes, Nina Simone did swing it on her first album, but even egotistical Hackenbush realized that she was close, but still not Nina fucking incredible pianist and singer Simone. Of course, Hackenbush only liked Nina's first album and refused to understand anything after it. But anyway, stripping "Love Me or Leave Me" down to the bones of just her and Cody would have been risky for anyone but her and Cody. She figured she'd sing it more or less straight and let Cody weave a counter-point-like accompaniment around the melody. Having just those two elements for most of the first chorus would give the song more build since she couldn't give it the denser sonic environment or something. She'd see how they felt about the melody after Phil and Ross soloed, they usually did something interesting enough to embellish upon.

With the "Love Me or Leave Me" issue settled, she made her way to the dump Shorty happened to be living in at the moment. Hackenbush never knew what Shorty lived on, he just seemed to exist, be beautifully dressed, and cheerfully optimistic, and had been so since she met him on a gig several years ago. He'd eventually convinced her to dance with him and Hackenbush and Smith had joined forces with the Eddy Lee Trio to become *Dr. Hackenbush and her Orchestra*.

They never talked about Eddy, except once, when Hackenbush was mellow on gin and she said she was sorry she'd ever met the bastard. Shorty was quiet, too quiet, so she asked what him what he was thinking. He said he thought she was suffering the same amount as she was happy.

"What?" she asked.

"You were so happy," he said. "And no matter how much you hurt now, at least you were so happy once. Nobody can take that away from you, Mabel. You really loved him and it didn't work out, but nobody can take that love you had, and the love you're capable of away from you. So I'm not sorry you loved Eddy, I'm just sorry he walked out on you. Does that make sense?"

"Yeah, kind of," she said.

They never talked about it again. They danced, they rehearsed with the band, they ate in cheap restaurants, went to art openings, the library, free theater events and parties together, took care of each other through thick and thin, but they never talked about Eddy Lee again. They never talked about love again either, mainly because the subject just never came up. Hackenbush healed up, sealed up, and worked off her passions through her music. Shorty had no shortage of boyfriends, some more generous than others, but, as far as Hackenbush knew, no deep and abiding love.

At that time he was between men, broke, but his sunny disposition betrayed not a hint of anxiety about either condition. And when she got to his place, a seedy bachelor apartment in East Hollywood, he greeted her with a festive plate of chocolate chip cookies resplendent in sparkles, pecans, and M&Ms.

She handed him his envelope of money and glanced around the shabby little room. "Is this charcoal of you new?" she asked, strolling over to examine at a tasteful nude study of Shorty.

"I modeled at Otis last week," he said from the negligible kitchenette; it was more like a kitchen-alcovette. Hackenbush didn't have to watch to know he was stashing the cash in a coffee can, under some ancient grounds. "The instructor gave that to me."

Hackenbush sussed out the signature in the lower left, and gave a low whistle. The artist was a woman whose work sold for tens of thousands, but who taught because she loved it. Hackenbush knew about her from her artist friends, who'd studied with her and had probably recommended Shorty as a model. "You should consider selling this," she said.

"It was a gift," Shorty said simply, and closed down that avenue of discussion.

"Then you should model more." Hackenbush headed down another conversational alley. "This is lovely. It's not all the artist; a lot of it's the model."

"I don't like being still like that for that long," Shorty said vaguely.

Hackenbush dropped it, realizing that Shorty probably overrode his natural modesty and took the job because he was very broke. She shrugged, and they sat down to one of the best breakfasts she'd ever had for dinner. "That was great."

"Thank you. I was going to cook this for Ross this morning, but Samuel gave me a lift home," he said. They shared the last cookie for dessert.

"Sam's a great guy."

"Yeah, he told me basically what happened last night." He gave her a searching look. You're okay, right?" he asked for the third time that day.

"I'm still okay, Shorty, and partly because Sam's a great guy," she said. "He kept his head and kept me safe, pal. I've never been in the same room with guns firing, it was confusing, I might've run toward it not away from it, if Sam wasn't there. I thought I could handle anything. Shows you what I know."

"Don't be hard on yourself, dearie." Shorty patted her hand. "You're not a gunslinger or a marine or something like that."

She laughed. Shorty made them a pot of weak mint tea, and Hackenbush made a mental note to buy him a box of teabags next time she went shopping.

She made another mental note to call caterers and clubs to scare up another gig that included dancing for *Dr. Hackenbush and her Orchestra*. "You're okay, aren't you, Shorty?" she asked, trying to sound cool, and failing.

"Sure! I wasn't in a shoot-out last night, you know," he teased.

"I know... I mean..."

He reached across the scratched-up nightstand that doubled as a coffee table, patted her hand, and got serious, "Hackenbush, I'm okay. I'll make you a deal, though, if it makes you feel better. If I'm not okay, I'll tell you right away, okay? Deal?"

"Okay, pal. Deal!" She put out her hand and they shook on it.

"And you, too, okay? You'll tell me when you're not okay, got it?"

"Oh, Shorty, I will, you can count on it!" She smiled and lied, knowing she'd never dump her troubles on Shorty. He was stronger than he looked, but she'd seen him suffer with her through the Eddy Lee break-up, and though she was willing to share her minor woes and irritations with him, she'd keep the heavy stuff to herself. Shorty was made for smiling and laughing; Hackenbush did her best to see him like that as often as possible. "So! What should we do now?" she asked brightly.

"I dunno know about you, Hackenbush, but I have a date!"

She was home alone with a book by nine. "Why do I worry about that man?" she asked Inspector Maigret, her favorite fictional Paris policeman, about Shorty. "He's just too cute to fail, isn't he?" She considered calling Anna, but she'd see her the next day. She ran her mind over her other pals, but then again, she'd rather not admit she was home and bored enough to talk on the phone. She went back to her Maigret mystery, once again marveling at how noble and human Simenon wrote his policemen. He made the bad guys human, too, but still bad or nuts, and still needing to be caught by Maigret and brought to justice. She'd read a lot of these books and also liked the way he wrote Inspector Maigret's wife. The Maigrets had a good, solid marriage; too bad that only happened in books, eh?

She got to Anna's office at 11 and found Dina Lee at the front desk with a pretty black lady and a prettier little girl. All three looked up from the computer with such polite, professional courtesy, Hackenbush was almost sorry she'd interrupted whatever they were doing. However, Anna called her into her office before she could think up a witty apology.

"I see Dina's coming along," Hackenbush said pleasantly. "Aren't there labor laws about teaching children word processing?"

"It's Lotus 1-2-3," Anna said briskly. She waved her guest into a chair. "And that's Alice Jackson." She looked Hackenbush in the eye and waited.

Hackenbush gazed blandly back for a beat or two, to see if she had more to say. "That's nice," she finally said, offering Anna a Pall Mall and lighting one for herself. "Where're we having lunch?"

"I said, that's Alice Jackson." Anna blew out a lungful of smoke and picked a shred of tobacco off her tongue. She made a face. "I don't know how you smoke these."

"The less initiated have been known to use a cigarette holder," Hackenbush murmured. She looked relaxed, but was frantically trying to figure out who

Alice Jackson was and why Anna thought she knew. "Okay, I give: who's Alice Jackson?"

"She's Tim Jackson's widow and that's their little girl, Alicia."

It was Hackenbush's turn to stare. "What's Mrs. Jackson doing here, Anna?"

"Learning a skill to support herself and her child with, Mabel." Anna looked out the window.

"You mean that child out there?" Hackenbush asked, tilting her chin at the outer office.

Anna patted her immaculate blond coiffure. "Day care is expensive. And I like babies. Don't you?"

Hackenbush decided to pass on the usual culinary rejoinder and just said it depended on the baby. "But that one looked pretty cute." She smiled and started to get up. "Let's go to lunch!"

"I have to talk to you."

Anna's voice was dead, flat dead; Hackenbush had never heard her sound like that before. She eased her flanks back into the chair and put on her listening face. Not that she needed it; Anna stared out the window for most of the conversation.

"I... I think I'm responsible for Tim's death," Anna finally said. "I asked him to stay another day, finish the week, when he said he felt very uncomfortable at Monroe Insurance."

"It's not your fault, Anna," Hackenbush said, wondering where that crazy idea came from. "Going into the park killed him, not the job."

"I tried to talk to the police, but they wouldn't listen," Anna went on, still staring out the window. "They even sent a uniform, Officer Brown, to tell me to stop bugging them, that they only had seven thousand police officers in uniform, including Chief Gates, and they were working on Tim's murder as thoroughly as they could." She crushed out the Pall Mall and lit one of her filtered cigarettes. "I disagreed, I don't think they're working on it at all. They hadn't interviewed me, or anyone at Monroe Insurance, or the family. Nothing."

"And what did he say?" Hackenbush asked. Arguing with the police was not her style, in fact, she did whatever she had to do to stay the fuck away from the LAPD, but Anna might be able to carry it off.

"I didn't say that to him, I was too intimidated."

"That's probably what he wanted." Hackenbush gave her wrist watch a stagey look; she was getting hungry.

"But then I got a copy of the autopsy report and I hired Samuel Lowe to ask the police some questions," Anna said, scowling at the middle distance. "He didn't get anywhere either. He said the cops told him, not in so many words, but let him know that Tim's murder is part of something bigger, and for me to back off."

"Then you should–"

"Why? What could be bigger than a life?"

"Anna," Hackenbush said in her best reasonable voice. "If Tim had a drug problem, and went into the park, there was nothing you could do about it. The cops find bodies every day; one druggie more or less... I don't think it's a big deal for them."

"You don't understand about the drugs, Mabel," Anna said, also reasonably.

"Just say no, Anna."

"No. Alice showed me a copy of the autopsy report and asked me to ask the police about it," Anna said in the same level tone. "There were no drugs or alcohol in Tim's blood or stomach at the time of his death."

Hackenbush hesitated. "Maybe... he was on his

way to get some?"

"No," Anna said. "Alice says he never did drugs. I believe her. Ross vouched for Tim. I still believe that." Anna's voice was rock steady, but her cheeks were covered with tears.

Hackenbush had never seen Anna cry before and found it unnerving. "I can't help you with the police, Anna."

"No, but you can help me with Monroe Insurance."

"What?"

Anna let out a breath, but didn't bother to blot her face. "The owners still want the books reconciled."

"Oooh, no," Hackenbush sang. "Nooo, Anna, ha hah ha–"

"Hold on, Hackenbush, there's a good story here," Anna said, knowing Hackenbush was a sucker for a good story. She went on when she saw her audience was sort of hooked. "You see, Mrs. Greta Monroe's son runs it for her, I think there's an accountant there, too, but she and her sister, Gilda Gonzaga, are the owners. Gilda bought in after Mr. Monroe died twenty years ago. They ran it until the son, Gary Monroe, was old enough to take over."

"Then they should leave him alone," Hackenbush said.

"They were, and everything was fine, until a few months ago," Anna said. "Things got, what did Gilda say? Things got sloppy and confusing in the books, or whatever she could figure out from the numbers they were giving her. She said they said they were just too busy writing insurance to really give her accurate numbers. That's when she called me for an accounting temp. I thought a guy... a guy would be okay there..." She glanced up at Hackenbush. "I met

Gilda at a Chamber of Commerce thing. She's lent me money and recommends the agency to everyone she can, I don't want to let her down."

"Did you tell her Tim got killed?" Hackenbush asked bluntly.

"I did, she's offered to help Alice and Alicia," Anna said softly. "Gilda's paying half Alice's salary here while she trains." She squared her shoulders. "But she still wants those books cleaned up."

"It's dangerous," Hackenbush said, half-heartedly.

"Don't go into the park after dark."

"Why me?"

"Because you're smart, tough, and I know I can rely on you," Anna said, as she had said in the past when she needed Hackenbush to bail her out of a client-related jam. "And you might... might notice something."

"Notice something? Like what?" Hackenbush asked. "Jesus, Anna, do I look like Nancy Drew to you?"

"Or not notice, whatever!" Anna banged her fist on her desk. "And Nancy Drew is younger than you are! Hackenbush! Can you please do this job?" She asked, switching from frustration to desperation. "You can do it part time, whatever afternoon hours you want. I've only talked to Gary a couple of times, but he seems nice, and–"

A soft knock startled them both. "Come in," Anna called. Alice Jackson, holding Alicia on one hip, opened the door half way and said Anna's next appointment was waiting for her.

"So much for another lunch," Hackenbush thought ruefully.

Anna said she'd be right there. "Look,

Hackenbush–"

"Well, Anna, it's been swell." Hackenbush started gathering up her cigarettes, lighter, purse, and jacket.

"I need you," Anna said, blotting her cheeks. "And I know about the Coral Cave closing. You need the money, and if you don't then Shorty will."

"Well, he'll probably have to take some demeaning job for a while," Hackenbush agreed. "But he can't do an accounting job."

"No, but you can, and I know you'll help him if he gets in financial trouble," Anna said, and made deal closing eye contact. "When can you start?"

"Never!"

"It's twelve dollars an hour."

"Really?"

They finally agreed on the next Monday, around two-ish. Hackenbush got a hotdog on the way home, but refused to enjoy it. Her only consolation was that Anna was cooking her a giant dinner on Sunday and doing her laundry for her. Hackenbush would also be returning the Lotus 1-2-3 manual she'd borrowed to brush up on the program; she'd gotten a little rusty.

On the way home, Hackenbush had time to mull a few things over. First of all she was still reeling a little from the idea that a woman blessed at birth with a name as fabulous as Greta Gonzaga would be fool enough to take her husband's name under any circumstances. But love made even sensible people do strange things. Further, she wondered if Gary Monroe had any deep-seated festering resentment that he'd been denied the name Gary Gonzaga, and all the attendant adventures and acclaim such a name would have brought him. Had he become a soldier, he could gone into battle screaming "Gonzaga! Gonzaga!" At least, that's what Hackenbush would have done. While the names Monroe and Hackenbush had their merits, she felt they would fail to strike terror in the hearts of their enemies. Or anyone, really.

Obviously Gilda Gonzaga was a woman to be reckoned with if she had the wit to keep her fabulous name intact. No wonder Anna admired her, and add in that she'd helped Anna with her business, there was no way Anna was going to let old Gilda down on the Monroe books. And Hackenbush, God help her, would be Anna's champion. Yes, it was stupid, but, yes, Hackenbush would do her damnedest to get the job done. Somehow there was a lot more riding on it than Anna Kodaly's honor; there now appeared to be a code of chivalry among LA businesswomen, and Hackenbush had been drafted. After all, Gilda and Anna were helping Alice and Alicia Jackson. Hackenbush would have bet money that Anna would help them in any way she could, but that Gilda was moved to help to help, well, that was most impressive.

Hackenbush found it all especially amazing since, due to the corrosive effects of the Reagan "revolution," the rich were getting richer and everyone else could go straight to hell. The bootstrap effect was only useful for destroying personal charity and curdling the milk of human kindness. Telling people who had no bootstraps to pull themselves up by what they didn't have was about as useful as tennis lessons for the blind and not much kinder. And this was not just in operation in LA, but internationally as well: every time she glanced at the LA Times or heard a snatch of news, it was all about the Reagan administration running amok in Central America, and lately in the Middle East. The Reagan administration selling weapons to Iran merely fed the cynic in Hackenbush:

it was just the kind of fucked-up mercenary thing she'd come to expect from those arrogant bastards. The stupid part was taking the money from that sale and giving it to terrorists in Nicaragua who were trying to overthrow the government that had replaced the former U.S.-backed government. Hackenbush thought the new government was legally elected, but she wasn't one hundred percent sure because she was really trying not to stay up on current events. What she did know was that her government seldom backed the right horse in Central America. Or Asia. Or the Middle East. Or, well, anywhere they could get their hooks into a bad situation and make it worse. Those who make foreign policy must feel dictators were much easier to deal with, except when they weren't, and were shocked to the core when those crushed under the totalitarian heel rose up and made changes. Apparently the American Revolution was the only revolution Washington D.C. would ever approve of, and then only the parts they liked. Hackenbush had no idea what Reagan had against the new government of Nicaragua except for the fact it was Communist. Her Latin American friends said it was Commie Lite, because all Communism meant to most people in Central America was making sure there was enough food and clean water for everyone. Hell, if that was Communism, then the Department of Water and Power was the Politburo and Ralph's Market was the Kremlin.

The whole subject was making her frown so she decided to concentrate on how wonderful she was to bail Anna out. Wasn't Hackenbush nice? Doing an accounting job when she hated accounting jobs. Brushing up on Lotus 1-2-3, which she also hated. Last time she worked at the Gas Company, she'd heard rumors that there was a new program called Excel that was much easier to use, but alas, it was only available on Apple computers, which were an exotic animal in most of the offices Hackenbush ever temped in. It seemed to her that Apple computers were mainly used by people who were afraid of Selectric typewriters and never had to do their own photocopying. In the mundane, get-it-done, workhorse administrative world Hackenbush thought she was liberated from, their yoke was the IBM PC; not pretty, but everyone knew what to do with it. Lotus 1-2-3 was the accounting software of choice, and even it wasn't so great; all it did was calculate, one had to use another program to print checks, invoices, and that kind of thing. But Lotus 1-2-3 did make nice, neat columns of numbers, and managers everywhere found this very comforting. Hackenbush wondered if management ever really knew how much can be hidden behind nice, neat columns of numbers. She'd been on a job once, covering a maternity leave, and found so many errors in the department accounts, she couldn't tell if it was incompetence or graft at work and she didn't speculate. The accounting manager hadn't speculated on what the problem was either; he just said he'd keep a closer eye on things when the new mother got back. And he thanked her, which surprised her; she'd been the bearer of bad news, it would have been more natural to curse her.

Yes, she was wonderful to help Anna and Gilda get the books at Monroe Insurance cleaned up. God knew what accounting horrors Hackenbush would find there, and there was little chance that anyone actually working at Monroe Insurance would bless her. But, oh well, what's an Insane Temp to do? Excelsior. Or something.

At home she glared at her laundry basket and decided to take a nap instead of doing anything else. Unfortunately she checked her answering machine and there was a call from her father, asking her to call him.

Hackenbush loved her father as well as any daughter of a second-rate Orange County woodwind player could. Big Daddy Hackenbush wasn't an easy man to get along with musically. He was very critical of his daughter and held her to a higher standard than he held himself. This annoyed his daughter no end, but she could never slam too hard into his musicianship, intonation or sight reading because, deep down, she loved him very much. He wasn't much, but after her mother left them when she was a kid, Louis Hackenbush was all she had. And he wasn't all bad; he'd given her her first baritone ukulele when she was a very little girl. He'd won it in a poker game and gave it to her as a joke, then found out it was no joke trying to take it away from her. She won that battle, and in retaliation Louis taught her to play the damn thing. Had he known the musical spark his mockery would inspire, and that his only daughter would surpass him as a musician, he might have ignored her and her ukulele. As it was, some of their happiest memories were playing duets and jamming with Louis' hep cat friends. But things had changed; Little Mabel grew up, packed her ukulele and moved to Los Angeles. Louis grew bitter and broke and angry at a world that didn't seem to care about regular guys like him. In the distant past, when he still voted Democrat and hated less, he'd been easier to get along with; the Reagan years had driven them even further apart.

But back in the present, Louis had heard about the shooting at the Coral Cave and wanted to know if she was okay. She put off her nap, and dialed his number, got his machine, but there was a good chance he was screening (they all screened their calls) and he picked up when she started to leave a message.

"Your Aunt Linda saw your name in the paper, are you okay?" Louis asked, or rather, wheezed; he smoked way too much.

Hackenbush smiled; Aunt Linda was married to Uncle Mike, one of Louis's old friends and she'd been like a real aunt to Hackenbush growing up. She was still one of Little Mabel's favorite people, enough that Hackenbush drove down there to see her at least once a year. She made a mental note to call Linda after her nap. "I'm okay, we're all okay," she said, omitting the damage to Ross' drums and not getting paid by the club. "Most of the shooting was outside," she lied.

"Linda said it was a drug shooting," Louis said. "Was it?"

"How would I know? I just sang there," Hackenbush said with more force than necessary.

"You're not on drugs, are you, Mabel?" Louis asked, as if trying to hear "drugs" in her voice.

"NO! I am not on drugs!" Hackenbush yelled at the phone.

"Don't yell at me, honey," Louis said in the most annoyingly reasonable voice. "You're awfully emotional alla sudden."

"Dad, I'm not on drugs, I swear it."

"Really?"

"Yes, really, I can't afford drugs," she said, knowing he would, on some level, understand this.

"Just say no, Mabel," he said serenely.

"No, dad, I mean, yes, dad. Hey, I have a gig tonight and need a nap-"

"You're not getting enough rest? Why is that?"

The suspicion was back in his voice. "Don't burn the candle at both ends, Doc."

Hackenbush took a steadying breath and blew it out; her father was the only one who could set her off like this. "No, dad, you're right," she said as calmly as she could. "I, ah, drank too much coffee last night and got up too early today, that's all."

"Don't drink too much coffee, Doc."

"No, sir." She nearly snapped the phone in half before they said good-bye.

"So, it was in the paper," she thought when she was off the phone. She knew Anna read the LA Times, so she called Temporary Insanity and asked Dina to keep today's and yesterday's paper for her. Dina said she would.

As worked up as she'd gotten at her dad, she was still draggy and managed a two-hour nap. She woke up thinking, "Who needs drugs with Louis Hackenbush as a father?" And this puzzled her out of her nap grogginess. She loved her old man, but talking to him could be as disorienting as smoking dope. Playing music with him was okay when they were playing, it was conversation that made her want to bite and scratch. Oh well, he stuck to gigs in the less affluent parts of Orange County and she stuck to whatever she could get in Los Angeles and the twain seldom met.

While she was getting dressed for that night's gig, she moved some sober skirts, blouses and jackets to the front of the closet. These were her standard office togs; not having a lot of money for day job clothes, Hackenbush had found a workable set of components in various thrift shops and consignment stores. She didn't have a suit, but she had enough jackets and skirts to mix and match that she had to be on a job a long time before someone caught on to how limited her office wardrobe really was. And then they just wanted to know how she did it and where she shopped to do it.

This was another talent she could, in a small way thank Louis for; after her mother left them, Louis shacked up with a string of women, most of whom were awfully sweet to his daughter. They taught her how to dress on a non-existent budget and carry herself so she looked like a million bucks. "It's not so much the clothes, it's the overall look," one of Louis's women had told her. And it was true; if anything, Hackenbush wished she was a little taller so she could wear more prints, but conservative cuts, good posture and an elegant gait kept her beyond reproach by being beyond fashion.

However, it was more fun to put on a little black dress, second-hand, of course, and sing in a nightclub, and that was all she was going to think about until she had to go to Monroe Insurance on Monday. At the moment she was more interested in her struggle with "Love Me or Leave Me," a struggle she planned to win that night.

Getting from Chez Hackenbush in Lincoln Heights to Alvarado and Wilshire wasn't so bad after midday on a weekday. It wasn't so great, but at least it wasn't rush hour. She'd agreed to do the Monroe Insurance job, and the afternoon into evening hours were just fine with her. Those were the hours Tim hadn't liked very much, but even Hackenbush was aware that normal people with families had different priorities. It didn't escape her that late afternoon and early evening were prime kid-playing-with hours and a good father would want to be there for that. And Alicia was, in

Hackenbush's admittedly uninformed opinion, pretty cute, too.

The address was on Wilshire all right, but it was east of Alvarado in an older building. Anna had warned her it was an "older" building, but that can mean a lot of things in Los Angeles. The elegant Biltmore Hotel was an older building, but so were the tenement-like apartment building wrecks in Westlake. In one of her rare forays into the Los Angeles Times, Hackenbush had read once that that area had a higher person-to-square-foot density than Manhattan, which seemed so incredible to her she'd filed the fact away and only brought it out at parties when the conversation flagged. These buildings were also firetraps and almost every year there was a big fire in a big building that wasn't up to the fire code. Those who didn't die in the building, died jumping from it. Just before Hackenbush moved to Los Angeles, Uncle Donald, one of her father's friends, had died in a fire at a place not too far from Macarthur Park.

So Hackenbush thought that "older" was Anna's quaint way of saying decrepit late 40s crappy modernist dump with a parking garage. It was worse when she got there; it might have been some kind of cocoa-colored brick, but the building had so many layers of black, gritty schmootz on it, it was just dirt colored now. There was a scattering of half-hearted graffiti on the building; the color and texture of the dirt made it a less desirable canvas. The schmootz was so thick on the bricks it looked like one could scratch designs in it, which would have been simpler and cheaper than a can of spray paint. Didn't LA ever clean their buildings? It must be possible; Hackenbush had heard wild rumors of such things happening in Paris, and if it can happen in Paris, it should happen in LA. As a bonus, the graffiti would probably come off with the dirt. The combination of auto exhaust and that creepy sticky black dust that came off tires or asphalt or both was no joke in LA. Never a clean freak, Hackenbush at Casa Hackenbush found herself pulling everything off her lovely white painted built-ins and washing the schmootz off of them and the windowsills with water and white vinegar every other month or so.

Very occasionally, in her rare fits of health consciousness, Hackenbush wondered what this combination of tire schmootz and auto exhaust was doing to her lungs. She once had the poor judgment to wonder this aloud in Ross' presence, and he pointed out how foolish she was to waste her precious time worrying about her lungs, because as long as she smoked a pack or more a day of unfiltered Pall Malls, her lungs had enough problems. This wasn't the last time she thought about her lungs and her health, but it was the last time she mentioned it in front of Ross, who didn't smoke, had never smoked and was never ever going to smoke cigarettes.

If it had any redeeming qualities so far, the Monroe Insurance building had a parking garage, which at least saved Hackenbush a little money. The other option was the RTD bus, and that was unattractive and very time consuming, too. Parking was cheap in that rundown, unloved, extremely dangerous part of town, but money was still money. She also felt her car was a little safer tucked away in the lot under the building. Well, not exactly under the building because the first of two levels was beside the lobby and then the rest of the parking garage was under that. However she was very happy to park in the visitor spaces under floors two through five.

Her mood didn't improve much when she parked; hers was the only car in a dozen visitor spaces. "Two in the afternoon and no clients," she thought. "Even I know that's bad." Sitting in her car, Hackenbush scoped the place out for a few minutes. It wasn't that she was waiting for the welcome wagon; over dinner the night before, Anna told her Gary Monroe and his Comptroller guy probably weren't going to be glad to see her because she was working more for Gilda than for them. It was on Hackenbush's shoulders to win them over with her professionalism and, failing that, charm them into submission. Had Anna not fed her into submission the previous day with home cooking—meatloaf, mashed potatoes and gravy, honey glazed carrots, and apple pie, and all of it absolutely delicious—Hackenbush might have quit the job then and there. But her laundry was peacefully flopping around in Anna's dryer, she'd just had a wonderful meal, and all was right with the world.

Since then, Hackenbush had slept well; she had a peaceful and productive morning, leftovers from Chez Anna for lunch and had thought about how to tackle the Monroe Insurance temp job on the drive down. Her message would be: I'm here to help you. That was all, and it was true. Whatever was bugging Gilda and Anna was not Hackenbush's problem; she was there to do the best job she could and that was all. It would have to be enough; she was through killing herself over day jobs. At least this one was part-time, decent dough and free parking.

So, all that being the case, she figured she better get out of the car and into the lobby. She'd parked close to the lobby door, where there was enough light to see if anyone was lurking. The garage was full of shadows and the ramp to the lower level was particularly menacing. Hackenbush figured you had to be nuts to park down there. Once she was out of the car, she noticed how clean the area was; well-swept, probably washed down, and not a bit of trash anywhere. Someone was keeping the parking area nice, which cheered Hackenbush a little; perhaps someone still cared about the place. The fluorescents lights buzzed happily in their fixtures and the glass in the lobby door gleamed invitingly. She locked her car and headed that way.

"Change, lady?"

Hackenbush had been so into her meditation on parking, she nearly jumped out of her skin at the soft voice to her left. She wheeled around, ready to fight or flee. "Fuck, you scared me," she hissed at the raggedy black man cowering in front of her. "Oh well, maybe I scared you, too." She adjusted her black hornrim glasses for a better look at him.

"Sorry, lady. Change?" he said again.

Hackenbush dug around in her purse for a dollar bill; she always had them from the club's tip jar. "Here." She held it out him, and took a closer look. He was small, but he was all bunched up in a crouch, so maybe he wasn't as small as he seemed. His clothes and hair were dirty, but his face and hands looked clean. He didn't meet her eye, except in short glances, but he said, 'Thank you,' when she gave him the dollar.

"Oh, you're welcome," she said, moving off, but keeping him in her peripheral vision. Most of the homeless guys she got panhandled by were harmless burn-outs, but she never knew if someday one was going to jump her. What she'd do then was a mystery. Ross once asked her why she stopped for those guys, it was dangerous, stupid and futile. She told him someday one of them might be Elijah and she didn't want to piss him off. Ross just shook his bald head at her and she had to shield her eyes lest she be blinded by the ebony glare off it. This always cracked up Cody, her bass player, probably because he had more hair, but Ross never found it terribly amusing.

When Hackenbush got to the elevator, she found a middle-aged Latino keeping watch on the parking area. He looked like he was in pretty good shape; he kept his moustache tidy, didn't have too much of a paunch and still had a full head of thick salt and pepper hair. The kind of hair Phil Noyes would never have again, if he ever had it in the first place. "Was he bothering you, miss?" Estaban Morales, for that was the name on his ID tag, asked her.

"Nope," she said, perusing the dusty directory set in a Formica case. There weren't very many names in it and some of the letters were broken. Hackenbush didn't know if this meant those businesses were still in the building or not.

"He's harmless," Mr. Morales said. "Can I help you find something?"

"I–" The elevator bell, which sounded like somebody drop-kicked a Chihuahua, cut off whatever Hackenbush was about to say. An elderly man, shorter than Hackenbush's well-proportioned 5 foot 6 inches, but with powerful arms, strode purposefully out of the elevator, nodded at Mr. Morales, and headed for the street door. The most striking thing about him for Hackenbush was the black eye-patch over his left eye, set off by his immaculate white smock below. "Excuse me, ah, Mr. Morales, who was that?" she asked.

"Oh, that's Dr. Abdurrahman Olldashi," he said. "He's a chiropractor. And you can call me Esteban, miss."

"Pleased to meet you, Esteban," Hackenbush

said sticking out her hand. "You can call me Hackenbush. I'm temping at Monroe Insurance."

Esteban shook her hand and blinked at her. "Oh... you do know about the young man..." he trailed off, still holding her hand.

Hackenbush decided not to play dumb. "The one named Tim? Yeah, I heard."

Esteban let go of her hand. "He was a nice guy," he said quietly.

"Was he a friend?" she asked.

"Not really, but he always said hello and was, well, nice..." Esteban stared into the directory before them. "Not everyone notices me and Petey, or speaks to either of us. But Tim always did... he was nice like that."

"Who's Petey?" Hackenbush asked, figuring how invisible a guy like Esteban must feel in his job and how far a little civility went.

"He's the guy you gave a buck to in the parking garage."

"Oh. I guess I should have introduced myself."

Esteban looked at her for a moment, trying to figure out if she was kidding. "Monroe Insurance is on three," he said, all business now. "They've got four, too, but the offices are three." He pressed the call button and waved her into the car. He almost saluted as the doors closed on her.

Hackenbush studied the scratched-up faux mahogany Formica walls of the elevator as it slowly ascended to the third floor. Technically this was only two floors, therefore only two flights of stairs. Hackenbush decided that in the future, she'd give her lungs a run for their money and take the fucking stairs. It would be good for her, physically and psychologically; much better than staring at

Formica so old there were patches of grey where the color had rubbed off completely. Hackenbush had a grudge against decrepit elevators. Growing up nearly poor in Orange County, she'd spent her share of time in Medi-Cal doctors' and dentists' offices. She couldn't recall any of the treatments being especially traumatic, actually they'd been as good as any she'd had in LA, but the docs were always located in creaky old buildings with slow elevators with scratched-up walls and faded, pitted linoleum in the halls. No sane person likes going to the dentist, but getting there pleasantly makes it a little less stressful, or so it seemed to Hackenbush.

So, yes, as she suspected, when the elevator doors finally opened on the third floor, there was faded, pitted linoleum in the dimly-lit hall she stepped into. "Why, I oughta make Anna see the kind of tacky joint Monroe Insurance is forced to inhabit," she mumbled to herself, peering at the dusty signage. "If nothing else, it would knock Gilda Gonzaga off her pedestal once and for all. What kind of philanthropist can't spring for new floors and paint? Christ, it's not like I want marble floors and murals, although that would spruce the joint right up. I wonder who Anna could get to do the murals?" She came to a door that had a wire mesh window set in half of it; "Monroe Insurance" was emblazoned on the glass in faded gold and black letters. "Ah! Here it is." She took a deep breath, squared her shoulders, put on her professional administrative office worker smile and knocked on the door. Nothing happened, so she tried the knob; it was locked. She tried all the doors in that hall; they were all locked and no one was home when she knocked.

"Great," she sighed. She lit a cigarette to help

her think, and then she regretted it. The hallway was old, but it was very clean and there were no ashtrays anywhere. There was a Ladies' room, so Hackenbush put her cigarette out in one of the sinks. The elevator dinged remotely somewhere in the building, jogging her memory that Monroe Insurance also had the fourth floor. She found the poorly-lit stairwell next to the Ladies' room. If there were lights, they weren't on, but there was enough light to see from big wire mesh windows that let in as much light as their schmootz-encrusted glass allowed. The stairwell itself wasn't particularly dirty, just old; Hackenbush figured the owners were too cheap to bother to remodel something no one ever saw. The stairs, moldings, and stair rail were wood; evidently this part of the building had escaped some misguided renovation project in the late 60s when it was believed Formica could cure cancer. Or was it that Formica lasted forever? Well, that certainly wasn't true, was it?

She got to the landing and peeked into the corridor. It was so quiet in the building, she felt like she shouldn't be there at all. She went up and down the hall; there were a few dim lights on behind the doors and all of them were locked. She peered through the doors that had wire mesh windows; the rooms were full of desks and filing cabinets. This hallway looked quite a bit like the third floor hallway, except none of the doors were marked. Now that she was thinking about it, only one door on the third floor was marked. No wonder the building seemed empty if two floors were more or less deserted in the middle of a business afternoon. Of course this wasn't the kind of building people would be inspired to hang around in; nevertheless, office space is office space and things must be very bad in Westlake if no one wanted any of the Monroe building.

There was another Ladies' room next to the stairwell. There wasn't a door knob, so she pushed on the Formica door panel. Not that she needed to freshen up, but she wanted to see if this door was also locked. It wasn't, but the light was out, so all she could see of it were dim shapes in the pathetic light from the filthy window. What she could see looked clean; it was the outside of the window that was filthy. Obviously someone, possibly Esteban, was taking good care of the inside of the building. Too bad Gilda Gonzaga couldn't be bothered to take care of the outside. Or maybe that was going too far; Anna said Gilda kept her hands off Monroe Insurance since the Monroe scion had taken it over. Anna said Gilda and her sister didn't want to crimp his style. "Tsk. His style needs its building steam cleaned and the windows washed," she thought sourly.

Hackenbush finished her inspection and took the stairs back to the third floor. Still no one around, so she went back to the lobby. Mr. Morales was talking to an elderly lady wearing a smock and wiping down the Formica surfaces in the lobby. She was wearing scuffed-up sneakers and had her faded gray hair pulled up in a tight bun; judging by the size of it Hackenbush suspected her hair must reach her knees. She gave Hackenbush a cautious smile and nodded. Hackenbush returned her smile and waited until she had Esteban's attention. "Hey, Esteban, have you seen anyone from Monroe Insurance today?" she asked.

He said, no and introduced her to the Formica-wiping Rapunzel. "This is Maria," he said. There was a brief exchange in Spanish, and Maria gathered her things and got in the elevator. "She's going to clean the Ladies' room on Three," he said.

"It looked pretty clean to me," Hackenbush said. "Just the Ladies' room on Three, not Four?" she asked.

"No one has worked on Four for many years," he said. "Monroe uses it for storage rooms."

"Ah." Hackenbush offered Esteban a Pall Mall, which he declined, and lit one up for herself. "May I use your phone?" she asked, and dialed the ancient rotary phone he pushed across his desk at her. "Hello? Dina? Is Anna around? It's Hackenbush. Yeah, hack-in-a-bush, heh, you saw 'Day at the Races'? ... Lola told you about it? How wonderful, some of what she said was probably true. ... Oh yeah? What else did she say? Oh, nothing else? Well, that's good. Is Anna–? Hello? Oh, Anna. Hi! I'm here at Monroe Insurance, well, I'm in the building, but there's nobody– What? Hang on." Hackenbush put her hand over the mouthpiece. "Esteban? Could they be at lunch?"

"I haven't seen them all day," he said, looking kind of guilty. "I thought maybe they came in and I didn't see them. They keep weird hours."

"Huh." Hackenbush shrugged and went back to her call. "I don't think they're here, Anna, Esteban hasn't seen them all day... He's the, um, guy in the lobby here... They did know I was coming today? At one? One PM, right? No, I don't mind waiting... The number here?" She held the phone away from her mouth. "Can she call here, Esteban?" He said, "Yes," and gave her the number, which she repeated to Anna, who promptly hung up on her.

Hackenbush handed the phone to Esteban. "She's not one for long goodbyes," she said, stubbing out her cigarette and wishing she had something to read. It wasn't that Hackenbush couldn't stand around doing nothing but looking so cool onlookers got frostbite, she just preferred to do it with a bigger audience. Esteban gallantly offered her a chair and that day's LA Times. Hackenbush graciously accepted both and tried not to scowl too much as she read through the litany of horrors on the front page. Reagan was still stonewalling Congress on his meeting notes, if he took any (Hackenbush wasn't sure Reagan could write other than sign his name on bad legislation); William Casey, former CIA director, was still dead, but the worst was some secretary with big hair and the absurd name of Fawn Hall had helped that nutcase North shred documents. "That girl is going to give paper shredders a bad name," Hackenbush thought. "I bet she's sleeping with him." There was a photo of Oliver North on the next page. "Ugh, maybe not."

She gave up on hard news and tried to read the Metro section, but it was worse. What happened in Washington D.C., or Honduras, or Teheran was interesting; but the crime stats for LA were terrifying. Murders! Arson! Zoning violations! South American businessman found murdered in Macarthur Park identified! After three weeks on ice, Mr. Jesus Montoya's body was finally identified. He was President of a small import/export firm named Sincelejo International based in Panama City, and there were no leads on his murder. The police were investigating a possible drug and gang connection.

"Which is like investigating that water is wet," Hackenbush thought. "Our cops blame everything they can't figure out on mysterious drug and gang connections. It makes them look like they're actually investigating, when they got nothing. They'd start investigating sunspots, if they could get away with it. They might convince the LA Times that sunspots done it, but the rest of the city would die laughing." She read the funnies and her horoscope before the newsprint on her hands started to give her the heebie-jeebies, and asked Esteban where she could wash her hands. He showed her a janitor's closet, but there wasn't any soap, so she trudged up two flights to Three. It wasn't like she had something pressing to do.

She was leisurely brushing her hair in the Ladies' room when she heard heavy steps and male voices in the hallway. It took her a moment to realize she was hearing Spanish, which she didn't understand very well, but knew it when she heard it. Hackenbush stepped into the hall in time to see the stairwell door at the end of the hall close. "Damn," she said, walking down the hall toward the elevator, trying locked Monroe Insurance doors, until one opened. "Oh, hi!" she said to the startled middle-aged man in front of her. "I'm from Temporary–"

"Insanity," he finished for her. "Ms. Gonzaga said they were sending one of their top temps to help us out. I'm Kevin Farrell, and you are?"

"Mabel Hackenbush," she said, shaking hands. He had a nice grip and a dry hand, his suit and smile were neutral, but she didn't feel any hostility toward her, just indifference and boredom. "I, um..."

"Maybe you could help us with a little filing before you get down to our messy accounts?" he suggested, and showed her a three-foot stack of invoices. "Some of what you'll be reconciling is in this stack... and that one over there, too. Oh, and the stack over here, as well."

He was gracious enough to let her put her things down and show her around the office a little. There was a square reception area with worn wood floors, faded beige walls, and scratched-up wooden desks. One of the desks had a computer and a phone on it; this would be graced by Hackenbush's lovely presence. Kevin's office was a few yards from her desk and there was another office that looked inhabited based on what she could see through the doorway. Hackenbush's desk faced the front door, and behind her to her right there was a dim hallway that Kevin said led to some disused offices. To her left was the file room that looked a lot like the file rooms on the fourth floor. She took a moment to get a rough idea of the filing system. If the drawers were labeled correctly, the cabinets were alphabetical and divided into Policies, Invoices, Receivables, and Payables. Hackenbush found a dusty plastic A-Z sorter on top of one of the filing cabinets and took it back to her desk with a stack of papers.

Hackenbush was a very meticulous and fast filer because she hated it very much. Using the sorter saved a certain amount of time and kept her off her feet a little. Aside from paper cuts, dust mites, being on her feet, and bored out of her mind, it was reaching and bending into drawers that was the worst part of filing for her. Sitting at her desk with a cigarette alphabetizing check carbons and purchase orders was the easy part. Mostly that afternoon she filed bills, receipts, invoices, and what looked like insurance sales invoices or receipts. She was hardly an expert in insurance, but that's what that paperwork looked like. None of the names were familiar, they seemed to be small firms, many with the words "import and export" in the names, and names like "Santander Trading Company" or "Amazonas Import Export Company." They were buying a lot of insurance, but it wasn't clear to her what kind. Not that it mattered to what Hackenbush was there to do. She didn't have to know what the numbers meant to get the books to balance; probably better if she didn't.

Around seven thirty, as she was thinking about putting her coat on and going home, Gary Monroe bounced in. Almost literally bounced in; he was tall, thin and way too happy to meet her. He was well-dressed, but disheveled and needed a haircut three weeks ago. His handshake was clumsy and his hand was freezing. But Hackenbush and her paper-cut fingers were on their way out, and after hours of handling paper, a cold hand on her tired mitt felt pretty good. Kevin had come to his door, possibly to do introductions, but Gary barreled ahead without them.

"So, you're here for Aunt Gilda?" Gary pushed his mousey brown hair off this forehead with a twitchy, broken-up gesture. His pasty face was pointed at her, but his eyes were focused in the middle distance behind her, if they were focusing at all, that is. He blinked a lot, maybe for focus, maybe because his eyes looked dry and sticky.

It was more of an accusation than a question, so Hackenbush just nodded politely. He was swaying a little in front of her, like a runner coming off an adrenaline high. And yet, he was so wound up, she wasn't sure if he was going to implode or explode. She dearly hoped if he was going to explode, he'd do it after she left. In the shape he looked to be in, one good sneeze would blast him to bits. It would be too bad Maria would have to clean it up, but Hackenbush was through for the day. There was no way for her to kid herself that this guy was on a natural high. She'd seen too many people wound up on speed or coke; this guy was so wound up, he was fizzing right before her eyes. "So, I was just leaving, Mr. Mon–"

"Call me Gary!"

Startled by this yelp, Hackenbush smiled reflexively as she flinched away. Not that he noticed, he was busy scanning her desk, the floor, the wall to her right. "I will," she said, adding "Gary" as an afterthought. Not that he heard it, he'd jittered off into Kevin's office "So, anyway, I'm leaving," she said to Kevin, still hovering nervously by his office. "See you tomorrow. May I use the phone?"

Kevin said, "Of course," and went into his office and closed the door. She called her answering machine, and found two messages from Shorty, one for a late lunch, which was moot, and the second one informing her he'd be eating soup at Astro's that evening if she was inclined to join him. Hackenbush liked soup at Astro's as well as the next chick singer around town and decided to join him, if some Silverlake Romeo hadn't picked him up first. Due to Shorty being long on charm and cute as a bug, or whatever that weird expression was, he got into good trouble more often than Hackenbush wanted to know about. Unfortunately the men in his life never stuck around very long, and Hackenbush hypothesized that it was because, being attracted to a choirboy, they were unprepared for the steely resolve and iron discipline of the dedicated artist under all the jetty curls, china doll complexion, and bug-like cuteness. Like Hackenbush, Shorty scheduled his love life around his artistic life and that, brother, was that. Art came first; it was the only reliable thing in their lives. However, the alpha males he got involved with never played second fiddle to anything, so they just didn't stick around very long. Shorty didn't seem to mind; there was always a new man on the horizon.

If Shorty's serial relationships bothered

Hackenbush, she told herself it was only because she was worried about him, not because she was jealous of his love life. In those immunologically troubled times, certain kinds of sex were killers. Prior to AIDS, the biggest worry for a gay guy was a bad case of herpes, everything else could be cured. Sex, as she recalled, was complicated enough: add on getting a medical history and getting the guy to use a condom, sex became an annoying chore, a tremendous risk and hardly worth the effort. Or at least Hackenbush thought so. She'd gambled on love and lost; AIDS just made the stakes higher in a game she didn't think she could ever win. So when she wasn't worried about him, she admired Shorty's courage and, she hoped, his prudence.

When she got to the restaurant, Shorty was getting appreciative looks from the clientele but no one was making advances because it seemed to be the couples' dinner hour at Astro's. Hackenbush joined him at the counter, thus adding to the mixed couples demographic; the room was fairly evenly split between boys with girls and boys with boys.

"I see you're much admired, but not likely to get invited home by anyone," she said, after she'd ordered coffee and soup. She lit a cigarette and picked a shred of tobacco off her tongue.

"I'm here to eat soup, dearie," he said, giving her an oh-so-innocent smile. "If I wanted romance, I'd come on the weekend and not invite you to join me." He waited politely for her to finish laughing. "Where were you all day? I called you for lunch, too."

"I know. I was working for Anna."

"Where?"

"In Westlake." Hackenbush didn't add any details because she couldn't remember how much

Shorty knew about Tim's murder and Monroe Insurance. She stubbed out her cigarette and stirred the soup the waitress had put in front of her. "Anna asked me as a favor and she knew I'd need money with the Coral Cave closed down." The minestrone soup was pretty good.

Shorty nodded; he knew from money, mainly not having much. "Yes, money, how annoying. I took a part-time job today."

"Oh yeah? Doing what?" Hackenbush crushed some crackers into her soup.

"Teaching the Lambada and Line Dancing in a storefront in Hollywood. The place is called the Dance Corral."

Hackenbush knew he could dance the Lambada because he'd tried to teach it to her, but Line Dancing? "Are you kidding?" she asked.

"Nope, I'm as serious as a heart attack." He smiled evilly. "I'll even show you my second hand cowboy boots I got the owner to give me. Strictly as dance equipment."

"Oh, never a doubt, Shorty, never a doubt."

They settled up, Hackenbush added eight percent to the tip to cover the Reagan waitress tax and asked Shorty where the Dance Corral was so she could see it.

"It'll be closed, but I have a key," he said. "Part of the deal is I can rehearse there when they're closed."

Hackenbush pointed her VW Fastback toward Hollywood. "This sounds like a pretty good deal."

"Oh, it's okay, until I can dance with you more."

He sounded down; Hackenbush glanced over

and patted his hand between second and third gear. "Hang in there, Shorty," she said, and cringed at how lame it sounded. Luckily Shorty was too polite to laugh in her face; he just smiled and perked up.

The Dance Corral looked about like any other dance studio Hackenbush had ever been in; hardwood floors, a wall of mirrors, a barre, and glaring fluorescent lights. Hackenbush had never felt comfortable in dance studios; they were too sterile and gave her the creeps. Shorty, on the other hand, had spent most of his life in such places and was right at home. He owned the empty space that Hackenbush shrank in. He'd been busy, too, and had worked out some new dances for them, and since she'd be working afternoons for a while, he was determined to get her while he had her. So, she danced, and danced fairly well for a woman who'd just spent four hours filing in a dingy office in Westlake. But it cheered her; the depressing dimness of Monroe Insurance had worn her spirit down and tripping the light fantastic to "Let's Face the Music and Dance" did her no end of good. She gave Shorty a lift home and said she'd see him on Wednesday night. Still feeling the dance in her body, she went home and slept very well that night.

The next day she was back, slaving away in the chilly afternoon light at Monroe Insurance. She'd arrived at two and still had to wait around awhile. This gave her time to give Petey some change and chat with Esteban. Without really trying, she learned that Esteban had come to work in the building almost twenty years ago, when Miss Gonzaga hired him.

"Miss Gonzaga? She worked in this building?" Hackenbush asked.

"Miss Gonzaga and her sister own this building," Esteban said with hint of pride. "They own most of this block. When I came to work here, Miss Gonzaga was helping Mr. Farrell with Monroe Insurance. This building..." he gestured helplessly at the faded Formica glory the entrance once must have been. "This building was once very beautiful and people were proud to come here. Now..." He shrugged and sighed.

Hackenbush nodded and pretended she understood. She was vested in no place; tied to nothing but her art and her circle, and both were highly mobile and constantly in flux. She could respect Esteban for his loyalty, but she wondered if it was really doing him any good. After all, Gilda Gonzaga had shaken the Westlake dust off her boots for greener pastures long ago. She must have, why else would she let the building go to hell? Why did she let Macarthur Park become such a nightmare, too? And while she was on the subject, Hackenbush wondered why the fabulous Miss Gonzaga allowed Ronald Reagan to become President and AIDS to run rampant? With a name like Gilda Gonzaga, she ought to be able to do anything.

This pretty train of thought was rudely interrupted by Kevin Farrell dashing in, apologizing for being late and dashing up the stairs, Hackenbush hot on his heels. Kevin was tending toward fat and Hackenbush smoked too much, so they were huffing and puffing by the time they got to the third floor. Hackenbush suspected they both had a competitive streak, because they were almost racing up the stairs. She thought that was stupid and decided to wait for him on the third floor or even the fourth next time he was late.

Hackenbush got down to work that day, which was organizing several stacks of deposit slips from the bank across the street. They were roughly in chronological order and secured with industrial strength rubber bands. The slips went back ten months and were for eight different accounts. Then she realized there were more than eight accounts and one bank; before she took a break, she'd found fourteen accounts at three local banks. This all might have gone faster if Kevin hadn't stopped by to ask if she wanted the window open, the light adjusted, a glass of water, the room warmer or cooler. Each interruption was politely declined and Hackenbush wondered why he was so worried about her at a nice comfy desk and had totally ignored her slaving away in the file room, mere yards from where she was, the day before. As usual, she chalked it up to the mysteries of masculine management.

Anchoring her stacks with desk furniture, Hackenbush got up to take a big stretch and quick stroll around the office. She'd been slaving away in the file room the day before and hadn't noticed a little kitchen tucked away at the end of the hall. Throwing a little overhead fluorescent light on the situation, Hackenbush found a vintage drip coffee maker, an empty working fridge, and a two ring hotplate on the Formica sink countertop. The faux burl wood cabinets yielded plates, bowls, a tea and coffee service; she found a stockpile of flatware, a whisk and three keys on a ring in the drawevrs. The room and its contents looked like they hadn't been used in years. She was marveling at how tidy it all was; perhaps Rosa wiped it down once a week, when she heard Kevin calling her name.

"Yeah, Kevin, I'm in the kitchen," she called. "Without Dinah."

"Oh," he said, peering around the room like he'd never seen it.

"Do you keep coffee around?" she asked. "Looks like a mighty fine coffee room to me."

"Oh... ah, I could send Esteban for some, I guess," he said, seeing the good sense in that. "Kind of nice to have the woman's touch in the office," he said, graciously, and wandered off to call downstairs.

"And cream and sugar, too, please," Hackenbush said, trying not to laugh. Coffee, chez Hackenbush, was a staple, and more often found there than flour or salt.

Twenty minutes later, Petey came timidly in with a grocery bag. He mutely handed it to Hackenbush and gave the receipt to Kevin, who gave him exact change for it, and retreated back into his office. Hackenbush frowned and asked Petey to wait.

"Here ya go." She handed him a dollar. "Thanks for getting the coffee stuff. Want to stay for a cup? I'm making some."

"No... no, thanks," he said, shyly looking around the room. "Thanks." He slipped out the door and was gone.

"Poor guy," Hackenbush thought as she put the groceries away and made coffee. Man, it smelled good. Not that she could smell that well because she smoked so much, but she could smell good coffee. She lit a Pall Mall to go with it and an odd thought struck her: Petey must get a bath now and then because she couldn't smell him. Not that she spent a lot of time sniffing homeless guys, but usually the aroma of sweat and stink of living in the streets wafted to her as she gave them her spare change. "Huh, maybe he showers at the Mission or something."

When she got back to her desk, she found Kevin on his hands and knees picking up the scattered deposit slips. "What the...?"

"I'm sorry, Mabel, I opened the window," he said, spreading his hands over the mess. "Cigarette smoke, you know. And these papers blew everywhere."

"Oh. I'm sorry, Kevin," she said, putting her cigarette out. "I thought I could–"

"I know I said," he looked sheepish. "But I forgot how strong the smell is."

"I'll take breaks and smoke outside from now on," she said, restarting her project that was almost finished. "Don't worry about this, I'll take care of it." She stooped down to collect what was left on the floor. "There's coffee, Kevin, why don't you get some?" she suggested when she got tired of his hovering.

He went back into his office. "Oh well, more coffee for me," she thought, grimly reorganizing the deposit slips.

By seven thirty, when she went home, she'd made twenty-two piles of slips for six different banks with offices near Monroe Insurance. This many accounts seemed a little odd; Hackenbush's usual experience was that businesses usually liked to bank with one bank, but maybe insurance was different. Kevin had gone out on an errand, so she locked the door behind her.

She paused on the stairs, listening to the building. It was very quiet at that hour. Even the street traffic was muted. No one wanted to be out and about in Westlake after dark. Esteban was in the lobby, sharing a Pollo Loco dinner with Petey. "Hey guys, that looks pretty good."

Esteban said he was sorry he didn't save her any. "If we knew you work so late..." he closed his ellipsis with a smile and a shrug.

"Heh, chicken from Chapalita up in Lincoln Heights has ruined me for all other roasted chicken," she said. "If they ever close, I'll have to start roasting my own own." She stayed focused on Esteban because making eye-contact with Petey seemed to make him nervous. However, she did call them both by name when she said good night.

Heading north on Alvarado, Hackenbush thought back over her experiences with the homeless of Los Angeles. She'd only had one bad experience; it had been at the Pollo Loco she was driving past just then, the one Petey and Esteban's dinner probably came from. She'd parked in the back and, not realizing there was a back door, walked through the parking lot to the street entrance. A skinny young guy panhandled her and she'd declined, partly out of being in a hurry, partly because she didn't like his vibe. Justifiably so: he walked parallel to her, screaming obscenities and threatening her until they got to the sidewalk, where he shut up and veered off down Alvarado.

Tough as she thought she was, Hackenbush was shaking when she got into the restaurant that night and slipped into the Ladies' room to pull herself together. Nothing had happened, but she always wondered what if something had happened, if he'd attacked her, was there anyone near enough who would have intervened? As harmless as Petey seemed, she had no way of telling what was going on inside his head. He seemed like a nice, burned-out guy. The kind of guy certain LA businesses kept around for simple jobs and maybe for luck. It was a good deed, a blessing, to help someone who needed it. A little kindness, a few bucks, and one solid meal a day were all these guys got, but it was more than the pull-yourself-up-by-your-bootstraps economy could offer them. She never saw any nice, burned-out women on these jobs; maybe they didn't survive, or if they could function at all, were bag ladies. Probably Petey was harmless, but what if he flipped out like the guy in the Pollo Loco parking lot? Would anyone be around to save her?

She frowned about this as she got closer to Sunset, where she made a small detour to go grocery shopping in Silverlake. To give her enough courage to face the market behind Astro's, and slightly kicking herself for not dragging Shorty along to keep her company the night before, she stopped into Rockaway Records to check out the dollar bin before she hit the market. They had Atlanta Rhythm Section's "Champagne Jam" album for a dollar, and she took it as a good omen, and even carried it through the grocery aisles as she bought coffee, cigarettes, gin, eggs, frozen lasagna, crackers, popcorn kernels, bananas, string cheese, a loaf of cheap wheat bread, generic creamy peanut butter and generic raspberry jam on sale. The last three were not for her sole consumption.

Wednesday was a gig night, so she'd made arrangements with Kevin to come in at one or two and leave at six. He hadn't asked why, he'd merely said Esteban would let her in if he wasn't around. Hackenbush took that as a vote of confidence, or that Kevin considered her harmless and inconsequential—either was fine with her. Before she left, she made a peanut butter and jelly sandwich, and carefully wrapped it in plastic wrap. She grabbed a banana on her way out. Adding a banana to her usual breakfast of coffee and Pall Mall Reds was her version of a health regime, and this accounting job was making her feel a little peaked. She ate it in the car on the way to work.

In the parking garage, Petey was waiting for her, but she was ready for him.

"Change, lady?"

Instead of change, she handed him the sandwich she'd so thoughtfully made for him. "Here. Hope you like peanut butter and jelly," she said, tossing the banana peel at the trash bin by the lobby door. A good throw, but she still missed it. "Damn, oh well."

Petey looked from the sandwich to her and back again. "Uh... thanks."

"Oh, you're welcome," she said breezily. "Have a good day. Oh, I'll get that," she called to Esteban, who'd come out of the lobby to either laugh at her poor aim or scold her for littering his immaculate Visitor parking area.

"Thank you, Miss Hackenbush," he said. There was a laugh in his voice, so Hackenbush smiled and waited for him to say more. "What did you give Petey?" he asked.

"A peanut butter and jelly sandwich from home," she said. "Don't get me wrong, Esteban, I like the guy and I think you're really sweet to take care of him, but two panhandles a day, five days a week is going to bankrupt me sooner than later." She headed for the stairs, Esteban's happy laugh ringing in her ears. "Oh wait, Esteban, is Kevin up there? Are you letting me in today?" she asked.

If Hackenbush had a code, it was always leave 'em laughing; and, as Esteban escorted her to the third floor, he was still laughing. "Fuck, I didn't think it was that funny," she told herself. "Maybe I should try stand-up someday." He was still chuckling even after he let her into the office and headed back to his duties elsewhere in the building.

Alone in the office, Hackenbush put her things away and found a stack of insurance policies with a note from Kevin asking her to file them.

He'd even put "please file them," in his note and she thought that was nice of him. Of course she'd file that stuff, but first she made a pot of coffee. While she was waiting for it to drip, she looked in the cutlery drawer. Everything was still there; she picked up the key-ring and tried it in the kitchen door. Two keys didn't fit, but the third one did. The coffee still had half way to go, so she went into the outer office and tried the keys in the front door. Same thing, two keys didn't fit, but the same key unlocked it. There was a janitor's closet near the stairwell, she tried the keys, and a different key opened it. It was a game now, and she looked around for other doors to try. She would have, but a chill went through her as she remembered something about a guy named Bluebeard, his bad marriages, and the perils of female curiosity. Or was it the perils of female sexuality? As a child, Hackenbush's mind had wandered when adults tried to tell her fairy tales. To this day she couldn't tell you how Red Riding Hood or Sleeping Beauty ended. She knew Rapunzel had long hair and lived in a tower, but not why. And that the chick in "Rumplestilskin" really couldn't spin straw or flax or whatever into gold, but Hackenbush had no idea who Rumplestilskin was, except that he had a cool name. But there was some bad business about opening the wrong door in Bluebeard's castle that nagged at her, so she tamped down her curiosity and went back to the kitchen. The coffee was done dripping, but first she put the keys back in the cutlery drawer, tucking them behind the plastic silverware sorter. They'd be easy enough for anyone who was looking for them to find, if anyone was looking for them.

She doctored her coffee with cream and sugar and took it into the file room off the reception area. It was more of a file closet, only four four-drawer file cabinets fit in it and Hackenbush had to stand to one side to fully extend a drawer, which almost touched the wall opposite. Good thing she didn't mind tight spaces, a tolerance she chalked up to driving a VW bug and living in cramped apartments for so many years.

Hackenbush had a theory about her life: events, emotions, ideas, luck of all kinds came in waves, interconnected sometimes, but in waves nevertheless. Today was her day for temptation. First it was keys and doors, now it was one file drawer at the bottom of the last cabinet farthest from the door that was labeled "Personnel."

Now, one of the cardinal rules of temp secretarying with any reputable temp agency was that every temp respect every client's confidentiality and privacy. Reading personnel files, however entertaining, was a major sin. Hackenbush had no idea if any other temps did it because if they did, no one ever admitted it, or at least never to Hackenbush. And Anna would have killed her if she ever found out. However, at that moment, consequences be damned: she was alone in the office and those files were irresistible.

Those files were also disappointing. Monroe Insurance had had very few employees; in order of thickest most faded files there was the founder, George Monroe, Kevin, and Gilda, who was a Virgo born in 1930 and a UCLA graduate in Business Administration. Also in the drawer, there were less fat files for three bookkeepers and two secretaries, a medium file for Esteban that looked to be in order, including a W-9 from 1984 to prove he was legal, even though he'd been working there for years. And then there was a very skinny brand spanking new file folder for Gary Monroe.

From what she could glean from George Monroe's file, which was bulging mostly with paperwork related to the purchase of the building, he founded Monroe Insurance at that location in 1953; at least that's when his yellowed W-2 form for the IRS was dated. Five years later he hired Kevin as his assistant. Kevin had only had two jobs since graduating from Loyola in 1956 with a degree in Political Science. He'd worked for Bank of America for over a year as a teller before he came to Monroe and stayed on ever since.

"Twenty-nine years in one place," Hackenbush mumbled, half in awe, half horror. "He's worked here almost as long as I've been alive." There weren't any payroll records, so she couldn't tell how much he was making after 29 years of service, but the most recent note in the file, dated March 10 of 1979, indicated he was making twenty-eight thousand a year. Hackenbush sat back; she knew legal secretaries who made more than that. Well, she'd heard of legal secretaries who made more than that, she didn't actually know any. On the other hand, maybe he got commissions on the insurance he sold, and, as far as Hackenbush could tell from the filing, he was selling a lot of insurance.

Gilda wasn't as interesting as Hackenbush thought she was going to be. The fabulous Ms. Gonzaga seemed to have come on board sometime in 1962, at least that's when she filled out a W-2 form and medical and dental insurance paperwork, which had lapsed in 1975.

All of their files were crammed with paperwork from the California Department of Insurance. Completed forms to be able to sell insurance, forms to apply for continuing education, forms confirming completion of that education, background checks, fingerprints, a nightmare of paper, carbons and fading ink. Hackenbush was amazed at the hoops these people jumped through just to sell life and property insurance. Was there that much money, love and fame in it? She doubted it, but perhaps they enjoyed it on some level; to each his own taste.

Gary Monroe was a different story: his file had his neatly typed employment application. He'd graduated from University of Southern California with a Business degree the year before and started with Monroe in the fall. There was a application for a course to get an insurance license, but no other paperwork, except a W-2 form which indicated his starting salary was forty thousand a year. The offer letter, signed by both he and Gilda, said he was the General Manager of that branch of Monroe Insurance.

"Fuck you, Gilda," Hackenbush thought. "Nepotism anyone?"

After learning that disgusting fact, which lowered her already medium opinion of La Gonzaga, Hackenbush lost interest in the past and decided to concentrate on the present and the future. After neatly putting the personnel files away, she freshened her coffee and smoked a cigarette in the kitchen. There was just too much old, highly flammable paper in the unventilated file room for her to feel okay about smoking in there. Back in said file room, she turned on an oscillating table fan some kind person had put in there years ago, and this relieved the unventilated problem a lot. She was filing receipts and boat insurance policies for companies with exotic names when Kevin rolled in.

"How's it going, Mabel?" he asked.

She noticed he'd helped himself to the coffee and hoped he'd left her a little. "Oh, okay. I'm about through with this." She waved vaguely at the stack in front of her.

He nodded and then took off for his office that had a window, which Hackenbush thought must be very nice because she was getting claustrophobia in the filing closet. She finished up post-haste and headed for the kitchen, where she found a fresh pot of coffee. "Men," she thought as he poured herself a cup. "Expect the unexpected."

Settled at her desk with a cigarette and coffee, Hackenbush was organizing her thoughts and the deposit slips when Kevin pulled up a chair. He had a fresh cup of coffee, from which Hackenbush deduced he wanted to chat. This happened to her a lot; employers willing to pay agency fees to talk to her. It was odd and she never really understood it.

"So, what is this thing you're doing tonight?" he asked.

"I sing in a nightclub," she said, reaching for her tote bag. She dug out a postcard Mr. Tanaka had grudgingly, but not cheaply, had printed for the band. The words *Dr. Hackenbush and Her Orchestra* were emblazoned on one side under a glamour shot of the band that made them all, except Shorty, look prettier than they were. Shorty was prettier in person, so the postcard made him look more handsome than pretty. The rest of them could use a little gloss and the photographer did right by them. The other side of the card had the address, directions, hours and a little map to the Lotus Room.

"Oh, how, ah, exotic," Kevin murmured examining the card. "May I keep this?"

"Please do. Maybe you can come hear me sing sometime," Hackenbush said. "The Lotus Room is a nice place."

"How long have you been at this?" he asked,

waving the card around.

"Since I was a kid," she said. "I've always loved music."

"It's nice you can do something you like," Kevin said. "So few people do."

"What about you?" she asked.

"Me? Oh, I'm not artistic or anything."

"I mean, are you doing what you want to do?"

He thought about it for a minute. "Pretty much. I've always wanted to build a business, not just be part of one. You know, a cog." He smiled at Hackenbush's nod. "That might not mean much to an artist like you, Mabel, but it meant a lot to me when I was your age. I'm very proud of helping build Monroe Insurance. Even though that doesn't mean so much these days."

He sounded so down on the last bit, Hackenbush thought it would be cruel to ask why. But, in the end, she couldn't resist, "Whaddya mean?"

"It's a different business environment than when I was starting out," Kevin said after staring at her for a few moments. "Ivan Boesky, for example, isn't interested in building a company, but he makes a fortune dismantling them. When George Monroe opened this office, it was to build a company that would last and prosper. Sure, there were get rich schemes, but they were small potatoes compared to what's going today."

"Isn't he in a lot of trouble? Like jail time trouble?" she asked. "I thought I heard something about it."

"Oh, maybe, I'm sure he has very good lawyers." Kevin seemed comforted by this idea. "And even if he does serve a sentence, he'll still be very rich when he gets out."

"Well, jailhouse ain't no playpen, but I don't think they'd toss him in San Quentin," Hackenbush observed. "What did he do, anyway?"

"He had information about the companies he was buying that he wasn't supposed to have," Kevin said. "Insider trading, they call it."

"Oh, he rigged the deck," she said. "That's what we call it."

Kevin wrinkled his forehead and gazed off into the distance. "Hard work just doesn't mean anything anymore, Mabel, building something so a guy like Boesky can buy it and kill it, why would anyone bother?" he asked... someone, he was so lost in thought, it was like he was talking to himself.

"Oh, c'mon, Kevin. Hard work still pays off. No one's ever handed me anything and I'm still here. I mean, we're not rich."

He started a little and gave her a long look. "No, no."

"But at least we're not going to jail," she said.

"True, true." He smiled a little. "But why aren't we rich, Mabel? Haven't we worked hard enough for it? Why does crime pay so much better nowadays? I suppose in your music field, I suppose the only way to be rich is to become the next Frank Sinatra or Barbara Streisand. If one has enough talent and drive, wouldn't you have attained that by now? And not still be working in offices?"

"Well, you got me there, pal." Hackenbush laughed; she wasn't sure that last bit was a shot, but there was no way she could let it go by without a least a little retaliation. "Here's one for you: why is Ronald Reagan still President?"

"He won the election," Kevin said coldly. "I voted for him."

"Oh yeah? Why?"

"I like his vision of America."

"Which is?"

"That this is a great country."

"For all of us or just for Ronald Reagan and Ivan Boesky?" she asked with the bland politeness she'd mastered over the years of having these kinds of conversations.

Kevin hesitated, then frowned, but not in anger; then he said something about his phone ringing and darted into his office and closed the door. Hackenbush had all the office lines on her desk phone and none of them were lit. "Poor guy," she thought. "Must be a drag getting sucker punched by the Reagan Revolution." Alone at last, she finally got down to work.

Hackenbush fired up the PC on her desk, and freshened her coffee. She would be entering the deposits into Lotus 1-2-3 spreadsheets and would need coffee for that. Lots of coffee as she backslashed her way to a reconciled, if not better, world. She sat down with her stacks of deposit slips and stared at them until she realized there was something different and counted her stacks: yesterday, she had twenty-two stacks, and today she only had twenty. She pushed her chair back and looked under the desk, then got up and strolled around the desk. Nothing.

"Hm." She drank a little coffee and mulled it over. Who would take those stacks and why? Should she say something? No. There was nothing she could do about it. The last thing she was going to do that afternoon was ask Kevin about it. She'd tormented the poor man enough for one day.

"Oh well." She'd worry about it later. There was certainly enough data to enter in front of her.

She found a directory named "recon" and opened it; it looked like unfinished reconciliations. A glance at the dates caused her to strongly suspect this was Tim Jackson's work and, by the looks of it, he had been doing a great job. Hackenbush had a lazy streak she hid by being efficient, so she copied Tim's format and named the file with current day's date. Following Tim's example, she continued to name the columns after the last four digits of the account numbers and grouped them by bank. Tim's spreadsheet had account numbers she didn't have, but that was too complicated for her to think about just then. She started to 10-key the numbers in, which was kind of a relief: something concrete to do at last. Hackenbush could do 10-key by touch and was really fast. Like typing, she could get into the rhythm of her work, but unlike typing, she only had to deal with rows of numbers and not someone's crappy handwriting, faded photocopies, or annoying voice on the Dictaphone. With the 10-key, it was just Hackenbush's eyes relaying numbers to her brain and down her right arm to her fingers. It was a kind of focused space-out and almost enjoyable, but not so zoned-out that she didn't notice Gary come in. "Hey, Gary." She hardly broke her rhythm on the keypad.

"Hi, Mabel," he said. "You are cookin' on that thing." He shambled into his office without waiting for an answer.

Hackenbush went back to being a focused, accurate and swift data entry Insane Temp. So focused that she didn't hear Gary come up behind her, or maybe he snuck up on her.

"So! How's it going?" he asked brightly.

"Gah! Jesus, you scared me, Gary!" Hackenbush's startled heart was slamming into her chest so she practically yelled this at him.

He laughed. Hackenbush thought that for a guy who'd dragged himself in there merely ten minutes earlier, he'd gotten himself a helluva second wind. "How do you like working here?" he asked.

"It's nice," she said, wondering what was up. "You know, part-time, free parking, good pay. I wish the account reconciliation was going faster, but there's so much to do."

"Is my aunt in a hurry?" he asked with a sneer.

Hackenbush decided the best reaction was none at all. "No, not as far as I know," she said blandly. "Have you heard different?"

"I haven't talked to her lately," Gary said, his sneer replaced with petulance. "She wants me to run this office, so I told her to leave me alone and let me do it."

"Oh, I see." Hackenbush lit a cigarette and picked a shred of tobacco off her tongue. Then she remembered Kevin didn't like the smell, so she knocked the cherry off and saved what was left for later.

"Aunt Gilda is bossy," he continued. "How do you like working for her?"

"I've never met her," Hackenbush said neutrally, and began hoping there wasn't going to be a messy outburst from Gary. "I just work for Temporary Insanity, but while I'm here, I work for you guys."

Gary didn't seem to hear most of what she said. "You've never met her?" he asked, sneering again. "She's a piece of work, my aunt. She never let me read comic books and only bought me educational toys when I was growing up."

"You seem to have survived it," Hackenbush

said. "Somehow."

"My mother always sided with her against me," he added.

"Ah."

"I wanted to go to art school!"

"Oh?"

"But I had to go to USC," he said bitterly.

"How annoying."

"It really is!"

"Well, your aunt must have some good points," Hackenbush said.

"No, none."

"Oh, c'mon," Hackenbush said cheerfully. "She's being really nice and helping Tim Jackson's widow out financially."

Gary got a very strange look on his face: half rage, half fear and maybe something else in there that Hackenbush couldn't figure out. "Oh... excuse me." He ran into his office and closed the door.

"I hope you'll excuse him, Mabel." Hackenbush jumped at Kevin's voice; she didn't realize he was nearby. "Gary was very upset by Tim's death."

"Upset is what I get when my voice breaks on a high note, Kevin," she said coolly. "I think Gary's more than upset."

"He's a little high strung." Kevin went into his office before she could say anything.

"High strung?" she asked herself. "More like highly strung out... and freaked out."

When she left at six, neither of them had come out of their offices. She shrugged and buzzed Kevin on the intercom. "I'm leaving." He said goodnight and she left.

Luckily, traffic toward Lincoln Heights was with her and she was mid-arpeggio when Anna called for an update. "What update? I've only been there for three days," Hackenbush said, applying foundation while she listened to Anna. This was the very reason she had a mirror over the phone stand and a collection of affordable cosmetics nearby; it was a time-saver for a busy woman who had to talk on the phone more than she wanted to.

"Well, Gilda Gonzaga–" Anna began.

"Gary says she's too bossy," Hackenbush said distractedly.

"Oh? Are you bonding with him?" Anna asked.

"No."

"Good. As I was saying," Anna said sternly. "Gilda was wondering if you'd noticed anything."

"I noticed the files are mess, there was no coffee in the kitchen and Kevin is a lousy tipper," Hackenbush almost snapped, applying blusher. "Ask her to be patient, I'll have a better idea what's going on in a few days." She picked up a lip liner and put it down. "I do have a question for the fabulous Gonzaga: what does Gary Monroe do there? I've seen very little of him and mostly he's very strung out on something."

There was a pause on the other end of the line. "Really?" Anna asked at last.

"I think so," Hackenbush said. "I've seen a few coked-out folks and he fits the bill."

Anna swore softly and said she'd ask Gilda. Then she said, no, she wouldn't fall by the Lotus Room that night, and yes, she'd see Hackenbush later. Her call waiting beeped, so she said good-bye.

"She called me from home for that?" Hackenbush asked her mirror. "Damn, that bossy Gilda woman must have some strange power over Anna. Oh well, maybe Anna's just being overzealous.

Or something." A glance at her watch told her she'd better hook it if she wanted any tempura veggies that night. The Storm Hill was pretty generous with the food, but there were more grains, tofu, and vegetables than meat or fish in most meals. That didn't matter because it was all so delicious; those chefs could probably make a banquet out of ramen noodles and saltines. She got dressed and finished warming up in the car.

As it was, she got to the club in plenty of time to have a leisurely dinner with Shorty and the band. Wang, the bartender, brought her a Ramos Gin Fizz in a glass the size of a flower vase and she was very happy.

"You look a little tired, Hackenbush," he observed with his superior bartender observation skills.

"Do I?" she asked, knowing she looked fine. "I have a temp job, so I'm getting up a little earlier."

"You could go to bed a little earlier, you know," Cody, the bass player, pragmatically suggested.

"I could try that, Cody," she said pleasantly. "I'll put on the same list as quitting smoking and drinking and driving on the freeway and–"

Ross' rumbling laughter gave her a reason to smile and look demure. She'd been working with these guys for so long, they knew how to bail each other out. Cody's frown only made his pretty café au lait face look petulant and Ross looked ten years younger when he was laughing at them. Shorty patted her hand to show his solidarity with whatever it was and Phil kept his mind on his dinner and the song list in his pocket. Early in his association with the band, he'd realized that the 'deciding what song to do next' discussion on gigs was going to drive him crazy. Henceforth, he drew up a song list before every gig. Then, at dinner there was a comedy show as Hackenbush and Cody took it apart and put it back together again with much wisecracking and music criticism. Phil was a great guitarist, and his job in the band was not an easy one, though he shouldered it manfully. He'd had a tough act to follow when Phil had taken over the daunting task of being Hackenbush's guitar player from Eddy Lee. She sang like a dream, but the first few gigs were rough because every time she looked at him, Phil could almost see the ghost of Eddy Lee she was comparing him to. This bothered him; guitar player ego or no, Phil was only human. He was also happily married, and Hackenbush—her talent, her temper and her sharp tongue—scared him a little; being the token straight white guy in that band was tough sometimes.

They had tremendous solidarity as musicians; Phil also had solidarity with Ross because they were both balding, although Ross was still miles ahead of Phil on that score, and because it was just a quartet, they had to rely on and respect each other. When Shorty was on the gig, it felt like a quintet because the dancing was so wrapped up in the music and was almost another riff on whatever the song was. They had a sound, a feel, a look, and when he was around, Shorty was just as much a part of that as any of them. Ross, Cody and Phil had never worked with dancers much, and had even looked down on them once upon a time. Shorty and Hackenbush had changed all that; they might not be great instrumentalists, but their musicianship could never be questioned.

One of the best things about the Lotus Room was the dance floor and that they were willing to pay Shorty and Hackenbush to use it four nights a week.

Wang had convinced the owners to hire the whole band, mainly so he could watch and listen to them until the cows came home. Or at least from nine to one, Thursday through Saturday. He was campaigning for them to do Sunday brunch through lunch, but the battle was far from won.

That night, like every night they were there, Wang did a bang-up job introducing his idol:

"And now, ladies and gentlemen, the Lotus Room is proud to present, direct from the middle class, the fabulous Dr. Hackenbush!"

He got such a kick out of it; it made him feel like part of the band.

And the band, for their part, they loved him back. They played and danced their hearts out for him, and whoever else happened to be around, but, at bottom, it was all for Wang (and the money [and food]). Every night was a good night in one way or another. It was wonderful to be so appreciated four nights a week; it made the rest of the week tolerable.

If Hackenbush had looked a little tired at dinner, she perked up under the lights, and dancing just gave her a charming glow. As usual, she sang well, but didn't find much inspiration in the song list that night. She'd been toying with a new version of "Love Me or Leave Me," but there was no way she could spring it on the band. And Mr. Tanaka, the Honcho of the Hotel Watanabe, was lurking, so she couldn't take any songs on a spin at all. Too bad, she was in the mood to take "Let's Fall in Love" apart and put it back together in a better way; alas, it would have to wait until next time Mr. Tanaka was out of town.

In spite of everything, *Dr. Hackenbush and her Orchestra* managed to have a good time that night. Even the tip jar was bountiful and the requests had been reasonable. Some time ago, after the tenth or so request, and just to be ornery, the band had learned "Muskrat Love," and Shorty even had a little solo dance to go with it. Strangely, requests for it tapered off after a few performances. They even offered to perform it occasionally and were offered tips not to do so. As far as the band was concerned, it was, overall, what the motivation books called a win-win situation.

Maybe she was tired because the last set was uphill for her. The band, and maybe Wang, were the only ones who could see this. Wang brought her a big orange juice and the band played more solos in the last set so she could rest. Not that she really needed to be coddled, but she didn't have to kill herself to get through the last set either. As they were packing up Ross asked her if she was all right.

"Yeah, I'm okay, Ross," she said, and lowered her voice. "Don't tell him, but maybe Cody's right and I should get to bed a little earlier."

"I heard my name," Cody said, materializing next to them.

"I was just saying how much I like your suit, Cody." Hackenbush had to raise her voice over Ross' laughing to be heard.

She went home, washed her face and moisturized, read for a while, and was asleep by three.

The next day she got to Monroe Insurance on time and cooled her heels in the third floor hall for half an hour. "They are going to get charged for this," she muttered to herself, looking at her watch for the umpteenth time. Bored, she wandered up to the fourth floor, just for a change of scene. She heard voices in the hall, but didn't see anyone, so she figured they must be in the file rooms. As she got closer, the first voice she thought she recognized was Gary Monroe, but he was sounding so stressed she wasn't sure. The other voice, sounding very stern but instantly recognizable, was Kevin.

"Where is he?" Gary's whine was almost a scream.

"Just wait and be quiet." Kevin sounded tired.

"Can't you send that girl?"

"That girl your aunt stuck in here is causing the problem," Kevin said sounding really pissed-off. "Get your aunt to get her out of here and problem solved."

Hackenbush heard heavy steps on the stairs behind her. "Oh fuck," she hissed, and ducked into the nearest open door. It was full of four-drawer standing file cabinets; Hackenbush wedged herself into the space between a pair and hoped no one would come down that far. The door at the other end of the room opened and the steps got closer.

"Oh, Christ," she thought. "How am I going to explain this?"

She could hear Gary laughing in the other room, and someone moving around in the room she was hiding in. Several rows down from her hiding place, a drawer opened and closed and something heavy thumped on the top of the cabinet. It was then very quiet, and Hackenbush got the panicky feeling that whoever it was could hear her heart pounding.

"Kevin! Kevin!" Gary was yelling from the other room. Hackenbush forced herself to stay calm. "Come pay this sonofabitch, will ya?"

"Coming, Master Monroe," Kevin muttered loud enough for Hackenbush to hear. He was closer to her hiding place than she'd thought. She silently thanked Master Monroe as Kevin left the room and turned off the lights. Crouched in the dark,

Hackenbush stood upright before her legs cramped on her.

There were footsteps in the hall and she nearly died when the hallway doorknob turned violently. She couldn't see it, but she surmised someone reached in and locked the door.

It took a few minutes for her heartbeat to get back to normal and then she felt stupid. "Why did I hide?" she wondered, creeping down the hallway. Gary had sounded crazy and Kevin sounded angry, but she could have just said she was looking for them. She shivered, the building gave her the creeps and if she wasn't doing this for Anna and fucking Gilda. "Oh well, if it wasn't for the Business Women of Greater Los Angeles, I wouldn't be doing this at all."

She straightened her shoulders and took off her shoes; quietly making her way down to the landing on the second floor, she put on her shoes and ran up the last flight and down the hall to burst into the office as noisily as she could. Kevin came out of his office, looking alarmed. "Mabel?"

"I am so sorry I'm late, Kevin!" She added a little dramatic panting for effect.

"Oh, it's okay, I was a little late myself." He looked at his watch. "Let's just say you started at two forty-five."

"Oh..." Hackenbush gritted her teeth and nodded pleasantly. "Let's!" To distract her from her irritation, she turned on the computer and made some coffee while it warmed up.

While waiting for the coffee to drip, Hackenbush picked up a small stack of filing and alphabetized it in the sorter in the file room. The third floor file room was smaller than the one on four, but it reminded her enough of it to make her tense. She could only wonder what the hell Gary wanted her to do and she was a little shocked at how exhausted and angry Kevin sounded, and how much he didn't want her there. It was no secret he didn't feel comfortable around her, few Republicans ever did, but he'd sounded so wiped-out that Hackenbush wondered why that was. True, he was getting as fucked and not kissed by Reaganomics as most Americans were, but Hackenbush and her ilk were still fairly cheerful about it. What could they do, but smile through the rage, keep working and hope for better days? The aroma of fresh coffee reached her filing dungeon and made her think happy thoughts about drinking a cup.

By the time she got back with a cup, Lotus 1-2-3 had almost finished loading itself. Happily, she got down to work because that was easier to deal with than whatever was going on on the fourth floor or how she was going to get Anna to pay her for the time she spent snooping around. She was flailing away on the keypad in a controlled data-entry frenzy, just Hackenbush vs. Lotus-1-2-3, when Kevin politely interrupted her death match.

"Sorry to interrupt." Kevin stood at the end of her desk.

Hackenbush gasped and thought her heart was going to barge out of her chest and slap Kevin's face. Out of habit, she hit the save key and took comfort in the computer's saving the file noises. "Oh, it's okay," she said with more cool than she really felt. She drank some cold coffee to ease her pounding heart out of her throat and back into her chest. "Ahm... I needed a break anyway."

"I just wanted to let you know that I have to leave." He had his coat on and a briefcase, actually two briefcases with him. "You can lock the door behind you when you leave. What time are you leaving?" he asked.

"Six."

Fiddling with the doorknob, he said he'd see her tomorrow and left. Hackenbush poured herself some fresh coffee and went back to her 10-key meditation. Her nicotine level declined to the point where she was disinclined to ignore it so she stepped into the hallway for a cigarette. The building seemed very quiet from there, but maybe all the Formica and linoleum muffled sounds. The third and fourth floors were mainly deserted; she had no idea what was above four or below three. In the time she'd been there, she'd hardly seen any other tenants or visitors. It was odd; the building wasn't any more horrible than its neighbors, but she supposed no one wanted office space in that part of town.

She was mulling this over as she smoked in the hallway, pacing its length, using a coffee cup for an ashtray. The Pall Mall was especially good, she thought that was because she wasn't doing anything but smoking it and hadn't had one for a couple of hours. But all good things come to an end, and Hackenbush stubbed her cigarette out and would have gone back to work if she hadn't locked herself out.

"Oh, this is so fucking annoying, I don't even know where to begin," she growled, staring at the door knob, unsuccessfully willing it to open. It was also annoying that there were keys to that door in the kitchen, which was beyond the locked door. "Fine, be that way." Her only option, other than break down the door, which she wouldn't do even if she could, was to go find Esteban and hope he had a key. If not, she had no idea how she was going to get home and to the Lotus room gig that night.

On the way down to the lobby, Hackenbush decided that Kevin must have pushed the lock on his way out. She'd have to be more careful in the future; the guy was very neurotic. She thought back on his voice on the fourth floor—it takes a while to sound that tired and angry, but being neurotic probably pissed him off and then wore him out. Oh well, so he had a creepy voice sometimes, it wasn't like she was going to be around long enough to worry about it.

Esteban was not in the lobby. "Damn," she said softly, tiptoeing around and peeking into closets. Eventually, she ended up in the parking garage, which also seemed strangely deserted. "Esteban? Petey?" She'd seen them both earlier, where the hell–

"Miss?" Petey leaned out of the shadows.

Hackenbush jumped. "God, Petey! You scared me."

"Sorry." He looked down at his feet.

"Well, never mind." She almost felt bad she'd been sharp with him. He seemed like a nice, very spaced-out kind of guy. "Do you know where Esteban is? I got locked out of the office."

"I think–" Petey started to say, but was distracted by a car pulling into the garage. "That's his car."

They waited silently until Esteban got parked and joined them. After he said hello to both of them, Hackenbush told him her sad story.

"I'll let you back in, Ms. Hackenbush, come with me."

She sketched Petey a wave and almost got a nice smile in return. "He's a nice guy, isn't he?" she asked Esteban's back as he led her to the maintenance closet.

"Petey?" he asked as he unlocked the door.

"He's okay, he doesn't bother you, does he?" Esteban took the solitary key off the hook on the door jam and relocked the door.

"Oh no, not at all," Hackenbush said, following him back to the lobby and into the elevator. "He's a nice guy, seems like he could live better than in your parking garage."

Esteban glanced at her and looked away. "I don't know, Ms. Hackenbush, people live the best they can, I guess."

On three he unlocked the door and they examined the lock; it was as she'd thought—Kevin had pushed it in before he left. "I'll be more careful Esteban," she promised. He told her it was never a problem and apologized for being out on an errand when she needed him. She said she always needed him, but he didn't really get the joke.

She spent the next two hours plowing through the deposit slips and still didn't finish. While the PC was taking its own sweet time shutting down, Hackenbush washed her cup and made sure the coffee pot was off in the kitchen. The dishes from the day before were dry, so she put them away. As she was putting the coffee spoons away, she checked to see if the keys were still where she'd tucked them away. They were, and she wondered if one of them opened the doors on the fourth floor.

"Well, that might be interesting, sort of." She shrugged and returned the keys to the cutlery drawer. A glance at her watch told her she better hook it. Running around the office she shut off the lights, grabbed her bag and coat, and made sure the door was locked. Out of the corner of her eye, she thought she saw the stairwell door closing, but she wasn't sure. The building was so damn quiet; it was starting to get on her nerves. "Don't be silly," she scolded herself, and practically ran for the stairs and screamed when she collided with Kevin on the landing.

"I'm so sorry, Mabel," he said, holding her shoulders. "I didn't mean to frighten you."

Hackenbush laughed, half in relief and half freaked out. "Oh, it's okay, I'm just, y'know, startled."

"Yes, yes, well, have a good evening," he gave her a fidgety pat and left her on the landing.

Hackenbush let go a long breath and rolled her shoulders. The light on the fourth landing was on, she wondered if he'd been up there.

"Fuck, who cares? I'm gonna be late if I don't get out of here," she thought, and ran down to the parking garage. She got lucky with traffic and was home only fifteen minutes later than usual.

Kevin leaned out of his office. "It's for you, Mabel. Anna from Temporary Insanity. Love that name!"

"Anna or Temp Insanity?" Hackenbush asked herself, but merely said thanks. She'd gotten to work on time, even started on time, but had been interrupted repeatedly by Kevin or Gary, who was really a pain in the ass, asking for photocopies, files, looking for coffee filters, and generally being weird and helpless men. Hackenbush had nothing against men, except the ones that annoyed her and these two were annoying her very much that day. So picking up the phone was a mixed blessing. "Hi, Anna."

"How's it going?" Anna asked.

"Fine."

"How are you?"

"Fine."

"When the sun is shining and it's not too hot, the weather is?" Anna asked archly.

"Oh, shut up," Hackenbush got her first laugh of the day. "To what do I owe the honor of this call?"

"I'm feeling reckless, so I thought I'd invite you for lunch or dinner this weekend," Anna said, laughing a little herself. "How about Sunday dinner? We can catch up a little."

This sounded a little too casual to Hackenbush, but she let it pass, mainly because she wasn't in a position to interrogate her. "Fine, say six? I'll help you set the table. But until then, why don't you drop by the club tonight or tomorrow? It's very civilized."

"I would, but I'm afraid I'll meet a handsome samurai and he'll carry me off to his feudal palace and you and all my other temps will starve in the streets. See you Sunday." She hung up before Hackenbush could conjure up a witty riposte. Lucky for Hackenbush; there wasn't much of any kind of riposte to that statement.

As she hung up the phone, she smiled at Anna's brilliant little dodge. All her temps thought Anna was a big square, until she said something so cool there was no answer, or did something so slick they could only look on in awe. Anna was as bright and creative as the people who worked for her, she just channeled it differently. She was more interested in letting others shine and succeed than making art or a spectacle of herself. Although in Hackenbush's case, she was able to make art and a spectacle of herself, and usually get paid for it, but she almost understood Anna's modesty.

But back in the bitter reality of her bitter day, Hackenbush began to form a bitter theory about the management situation at Monroe Insurance. Although she wasn't an expert on how offices ran, she'd worked in enough of them to figure out who was doing all the work and who was getting all the credit. She'd also seen some bad deals in her life and knew one when she saw one. But if Kevin was getting the shaft, he was certainly working hard for it. In the last year, business had, as far as Hackenbush could tell, tripled or quadrupled, and it all seemed to be in policies Kevin was writing. At least those payments in and payments out were the majority of what Hackenbush was filing and data-entering in the computer. The admin and paper situation had only gotten out of control in the past year or so, shortly after they'd passed their audit, judging by the audit report she'd happened to glance at in the files. She thought it was odd that they didn't hire a new bookkeeper and a secretary when there was so much work and so much money running through the place. It was probably just her annoyed state of mind, but she was even a little outraged that, with unemployment hovering around seven percent, Monroe Insurance didn't see fit to give two decent workers a permanent job with benefits. Not that she saw herself ever taking a job there, but it would have been a good job for scores of people whose acquaintance Hackenbush would never make.

Another thing that was pissing her off that afternoon was that she couldn't get her fucking checking accounts to reconcile. It was getting late, too, so her frustration was double. She frowned and rummaged around in the desk until she found a floppy disk and copied the whole directory onto it. She'd have a little revenge on Anna and make her work on this recon, too. On her way out, she made sure the computer, the coffee pot and the kitchen lights were off; it was Friday, after all.

Gary's office was dark already, as usual. He'd been a stressed-out pain in Hackenbush's ass for a few hours that day and she was glad when he skittered off. "Night, Kevin," she said, to his open door.

"Ah, that time already?" He got up and walked her to the door. "How's it going out here?" he asked.

"Okay," she said. "Slowly though. I'm having trouble finding a place in the checkbooks to reconcile to and my numbers aren't adding up in any way that makes sense."

"What do you think the problem is?" he asked, stepping in front of her.

Hackenbush thought he was more interested in this than she'd ever seen him. "Well, I think there are checks and deposits missing. I've been over the deposit slips and the cancelled checks, and there are more debits and credits on the bank statements than I can account for in the office," she said, looking up at his unreadable frown and trying to sound professional. "Maybe the banks are making mistakes. What do you think?"

He thought this over for a half a second and seemed to relax. "Maybe," he said, almost cheerfully. "Will you be back on Monday?"

"That's the plan," she said. He accompanied her to the stairs where he said he'd see her on Monday, and left her to descend the two flights on her own.

Half a dozen steps down the stairs, she heard the elevator ding, heard Kevin greet someone in English, and then someone else speaking Spanish. Just out of curiosity, Hackenbush went up a few steps to peek into the hall, and saw three men she didn't recognize go into the office with Kevin. She thought she recognized one of the voices from somewhere, but even her trained ear wasn't that good. And most male voices sounded the same to her when she was far away from them, so she was really kidding herself if she thought she recognized one of them.

That night at the gig, Wang made her a superior Ramos Gin Fizz and even let her drink half of it before introducing her mid-way through the first set. "And now, Ladies and Gentlemen, the Lotus Room is proud to present, direct from the middle class, the fabulous Dr. Hackenbush!" He had such flair, her one and only Wang.

She sang "Moonglow" like she meant it and looked around the room for the handsome samurai Anna was so afraid of meeting. He wasn't there; Anna's heart would have been safe that night.

"I love these bread dough vests you put on meatloaf, Anna," Hackenbush said as they sat down to eat on Sunday. "It's so... homey and bizarre at the same time."

"I only do it to impress you," Anna said, dishing up a slice with mashed potatoes for her guest. "I considered doing a bread dough bikini for you, but I think that's an idea ahead of its time."

"I couldn't agree more. Maybe next time you could do King Tut's sarcophagus."

"I'll give that some thought." Anna took a sip of the pretty good red wine Hackenbush picked because she liked the label and leaned back. "Tell me what's going on at Monroe Insurance."

"Eat your dinner before it gets cold."

"Tell me while I eat," Anna said and dug in.

Hackenbush shoved some food in her mouth to fortify herself. "Well, I think Gary Monroe is on drugs because he just ain't right. He's nervous around the office and not there very much." She took a sip of wine. A small sip; she wasn't a big wine-drinker but she knew it went with meatloaf. "The Controller guy, Kevin, is okay. He's pleasant, but I overheard him say he wanted me out of there ASAP. There's something weird with the accounts, Anna, more than just neglect. I can't get them to balance, I don't have everything I need to do it, and I get the runaround whenever I ask. I'm not pushing it, those guys are very tense."

"What's missing for the accounts?" Anna asked, while Hackenbush finished off her mashed potatoes.

"Deposit slips, cancelled checks, bank statements," Hackenbush reeled off. "I can't even begin to match the policies written to what might have been deposited, let alone what might have been paid out."

"You're not there to do that, Mabel. That's an auditor's job," Anna said, putting more food on Hackenbush's plate. "I mean, I think that's what auditors do, isn't it?"

"Why don't you ask Gilda Gonzaga?" Hackenbush liked the way that name just rolled off her tongue.

"I will," she said. "In the meantime–"

"Oh, wait! In the meantime, I brought you a disk of what I can't figure out." Hackenbush fished the floppy out of her purse and handed it to her hostess. "There's some of Tim's work on there, too. Maybe a better accounting mind than mine can figure it out."

"I'll show it to Dina. She's turning into some kind of number whizkid."

"Why don't you show it to Gilda Gonzaga?" Hackenbush asked. "It's her company, isn't it?"

Anna nodded. "About Gary... I think his mother and his aunt have been worried," she said slowly. "According to Gilda, Gary's been acting strangely for six or seven months–"

"That she's noticed," Hackenbush put in. "How often does she see him?" She helped Anna clear the table and serve dessert.

"I don't know, I can ask," Anna said, dishing up vanilla ice cream and canned peaches. "Gilda said it's been tense since she talked to Gary and Kevin about closing that office and moving it all to the main office on the Westside."

"Huh," Hackenbush said thoughtfully. "I think they'd hate that."

"Why do you think that?"

"Well, they might not be happy at that office, but they know it and it feels like its theirs," Hackenbush said vaguely. "I can't really explain that, just a feeling."

"I understand."

"When did the subject of moving come up?" Hackenbush asked.

"About a year ago..."

"... and shortly after that everything started to go to hell," Hackenbush finished for her. They stared at each other across the table. "I quit, Ms. Kodaly, I'll work next week for you, but you make Gilda understand that she better close that office pretty damn quick."

"She–"

"Anna," Hackenbush cut her off. "I don't understand what's going on there. It's strange, I never see clients. Seems like Kevin is writing a lot of insurance and paying a lot of claims, at least I'm filing new policies and deciphering checkbook entries every day, but where and when is he doing this? I really think Gilda should get more involved and find out what the fuck is going on in that office because it's more than I can figure out."

"So I see," Anna said. "Well, not to worry, Hackenbush." She reached over and patted Hackenbush's hand, knocking an unlit cigarette out of it. "I'll deal with it first thing Monday, you might not have to do the whole week."

"Fine with me," Hackenbush said, lighting up and leaning back with a cup of coffee.

"Oh, by the way, you haven't seen a yellow backpack around the office, have you?" Anna asked suddenly.

"No."

"The police didn't find Tim's backpack with his body," Anna added.

"If he was killed in Macarthur Park, of course not," Hackenbush said. "It's amazing they found anything of him at all."

"Really, Hackenbush," Anna scolded. "We just ate."

"Sorry."

Hackenbush was gifted with a challenging Monday. Both Kevin and Gary were in the office again, driving her nuts with interruptions, running in and out of the office, asking her to make coffee, copies, file stuff, and nothing she did was quick enough. By four o'clock, she was ready to kill them; by five she was ready to kill them and then kill herself; by six she was ready to kill everyone. Towards seven, whatever fine thread was keeping Gary Monroe together snapped with a loud twang.

"You want me to do what, Gary?" she asked the freaked-out pasty white guy leaning over her desk.

"There's a guy in the park," he hissed. "He has something I want you to get for me and–"

"It's dark out there," Hackenbush said briskly. "Forget it."

"I really need–"

"No."

"I'm telling you–" Gary's voice was rising to a scream.

"And I said, no." Hackenbush got up and faced off with him.

Kevin came out of this office. "What's going on?" he asked, looking alarmed.

"Insubordination," Hackenbush said snappily. "And now I'm getting some coffee." She turned on her heel and marched down to the kitchen. Gary was right behind her, yelling now.

"You bitch! How dare you–"

"I'm not going into Macarthur Park after dark to score you drugs, asshole, get it?" Hackenbush yelled back, picking up the half-full coffeepot.

"Wait, wait–" Kevin was practically prancing between them. "Hackenbush, maybe you should leave?"

"Sounds good to me," she said. Half turned to dump the pot in the sink, she dodged the swing Gary took at her. Kevin seemed rooted to the spot, so she threw the contents of the pot in Gary's face. He screamed and ran out of the room.

"Jesus, Mabel!" Kevin ran after the younger man.

Hackenbush let out the breath she'd been holding. "Oh please, it wasn't that hot," she murmured, touching the pot to her palm. No, not too hot; out of habit she turned off the coffee maker and put the empty pot in the dish drainer. She was shaking and took a few more breaths to get herself under control. Her eye fell on the cutlery drawer, the drawer with the keys that might open doors on the fourth floor. She dug out the key ring and pocketed the keys. There was no reason to believe any of these keys would fit doors on the fourth floor, but it was worth a try. She heard footsteps in the hall and hoped to God it was Kevin; she was out of warm-to-hot coffee weapons and had lost the element of surprise.

Kevin leaned in the doorway, gray-faced. "Are you okay?" he asked.

"Yeah, but what the fuck is with him?"

"Drugs." Kevin looked tired, dead tired. "Gary's been struggling with a coke addition for quite a while now. I thought he had it under control." They stared at each other for a few seconds, until Hackenbush looked away.

"Kevin, this has to be my last day, sorry," she said, brushing past him. "I'll get my time card ready."

He followed her out to her desk and signed the card while she shut down the PC. "Sorry, Hackenbush," he said. "I have a client in a few minutes, but after that, I think I'll call it a day, too."

"Kind of late for clients, isn't it, Kevin?" she asked.

Kevin shrugged. "Some businessmen only have time at the end of a long day," he said vaguely. He looked really old and really tired.

They shook hands, Hackenbush picked up her tote bag, and she suddenly felt sorry for the guy. "Hey, Kevin," she said cheerfully. "How 'bout I make one last pot of coffee before I go?"

"You don't have to."

"How late will you be here?"

"A couple of more hours," he said. "It would be nice though, to have some coffee when the clients get here."

"Say no more!" She put her things down and marched into the kitchen. Whatever was going on, Kevin was one unhappy guy, so Hackenbush figured this one small kindness wouldn't kill her. As she made the coffee, she considered putting the keys back in the drawer and forgetting about everything. This was Gilda's problem, let her solve it. She was distracted by voices in the outer office. The coffee was dripping; her work was done there. She'd just be on her way, but as she came to the outer office, she came face to face with Mr. Bob Jones X and three of his thugs.

"Oh, Hackenbush..." The idiot just stood there staring at her. As Hackenbush recalled, he never was very good with surprises. Neither was she.

"Oh shit, not you." She covered her eyes, hoping he'd be gone when she uncovered them. No luck there.

Kevin looked from one to the other; he wasn't doing very well with this surprise either. "Uh... do you know each other?"

"Yeah, we kind of know each other," Hackenbush said, figuring some riff on the truth was her best bet. "He likes the way I sing."

"Oh yes, very much, very much," Bob said, recovering a little. "You were magnificent at the Coral Cave, Hackenbush, truly magnificent."

"I'm always magnificent, Bob," she said, picking up her tote bag. "And now I must go."

"Do they have it?" Gary's strangled voice came from behind the wall of thugs behind Bob. "Is that cunt still here," he asked, glaring at Hackenbush when the thugs parted and he could see her.

"What the–?" Bob was surprised again.

"He's talking about me," Hackenbush whispered. "Well, I must go."

"Do they have it? Gary was starting to sound desperate. Still coffee stained, he was staring at Hackenbush like a crazy man.

It occurred to Hackenbush that there wasn't anything between her and Gary, and no telling what

Bob or Kevin would do in this situation. She figured the thugs would do what Bob told them.

"Gary, I–" Kevin started to move toward him, putting himself in Gary's path to Hackenbush. He was almost where he could so some good when Gary screamed and lunged for Hackenbush.

One of Bob's thugs grabbed him by the coat and pinned him to the wall. He looked at Bob for instructions. Bob looked at Hackenbush, who looked at her watch.

"Well," she said, taking a big step around Gary and the thug holding him. "Good-bye!"

"Wait, Hackenbush!" Bob was on her heels as she made for the stairs. Bob's thugs were behind him and somewhere behind them were Kevin and Gary.

"No time, Bob," she said plunging into hall and heading for the stairwell.

"It's been years since we talked, Hackenbush," he said behind her.

"We just talked on the phone," she said rounding the landing between three and two. "Have you forgotten already?"

"No, no, no," he said quickly. "But that wasn't a very good talk."

"There are no good talks for us, Bob," she said.

"Hackenbush, you know I've always admired you," he said, starting to sound winded.

"Yes, yes, yes," she said quickly.

"Things have changed in my life. I think it could work out for us now," he said. "If you'd just give it another try."

"Forget it, Bob," she said. "My career is at a place where I can't be swept up in a DEA raid or die in a hail of bullets."

"That would never happen!"

"Says you."

"Hackenbush, I think you could... you could," he seemed to be faltering. "I think you could save me from myself."

Hackenbush flung open the lobby door and waved at Esteban and Maria. "I could never do that, Bob," she said, turning to face him. "It's much too dangerous." She swept into the parking garage and found two thugs beating up Petey. Bob's swarthy companion at the Coral Cave sat on a car fender, looking on. He rose to his feet and bowed at the sight of Hackenbush. This was lost on her as she turned to scream at the thugs. "Stop it! Stop it!" This didn't work, so she screamed at Bob. "Do something! Make them stop."

"Oh, now I have your attention," he said, examining his nails.

"Goddam you, Bob, stop them! You owe me! I saved your fucking life!"

"That was quite a while ago," Bob drawled. "What have you done for me lately?"

"You're fucking alive lately because I told the killers you weren't in your apartment, when you were." Hackenbush was snarling; she hated snarling. "Then I gave you fifty bucks and a ride to the Greyhound to get out of town. I even got rid of your junker car for you. Now call off your thugs!"

"Miguel, por favor?" Bob called to the well-dressed swarthy man by the car, who snapped his fingers and the thugs moved to his side.

Hackenbush shoved past Bob, Kevin, Gary, and Bob's thugs and waved Maria and Esteban into the garage. They looked scared but they came and picked up Petey.

"They said he's a cop," Bob told her.

"Oh, Bob," she sighed. "Return to earth. He's a homeless guy."

The swarthy guy said something in Spanish to Bob. "Miguel says he enjoyed your singing at the Coral Cave," Bob said.

"Oh thank you." She nodded in Miguel's general direction. "Will you please go away now?"

"Get the car," he said.

"But Mr. Jones!" Kevin looked a little panicked.

"I think I won't buy any insurance tonight, Kev," Bob said, his voice like a knife. "Sorry." Kevin practically ran out of the garage.

Bob put his hands on Hackenbush's shoulders. "I guess there's nothing to say," he said, and continued. "We live in different worlds. Mine is full of international travel, fine food, clothes, five-star hotels. And yours is... um, whatever it is."

"Yeah, yeah, yeah, Bob, see ya," she said, slipping out from under his hands.

He turned to go, and turned back. "Hackenbush, why not?" he asked.

"Because bad things happen where you are, Bob," she said coldly. "And it's so nice to know respectable people instead of drug addled scum, like when I knew you. Seeing you here tonight was an accident–"

"Fate! Kismet!"

"No. An accident, maybe a curse, but now it's over," she said. "I saved your life, and you just did me a favor. We're not even, and since you still owe me, I want you to stay away from me."

"I owe you?" he snorted, now that he knew his jig was up. "What about that money I sent you?"

"What about that the club got shot up because of you and your, ah, business connections?" she shot back. "Just go, Bob, before, by some incredible miracle, I find it possible to think even less of you."

He squared his shoulders and walked away from her. Gary ran up to him, and started to say something. Bob backhanded him and said, "Get it in the park."

Hackenbush was in the lobby before the caravan of thugs left the building. Petey was a bloody mess. "God, Esteban, is he okay?" she asked.

"He needs a doctor, a hospital." He and Maria were doing the best they could with a little first aid box, the kind you buy at the drugstore.

"No hospital," Petey moaned. "No doctor."

The elevator dinged softly and a man wearing a black eye patch over his left eye stepped out of it. "Good God, what happened?" he said, rushing up to Petey.

"Dr. Olldashi!" Esteban said. "Can you help us?"

"He won't go to the hospital," Hackenbush said lamely. She was trying to remember what Dr. Olldashi did. Oh yes, he was a chiropractor; that might do some good.

"Well, bring him up to my office," Dr. Olldashi said. They all got into the elevator with the protesting Petey. It was kind of a tight squeeze, but Dr. Olldashi's office was on the second floor, so not a long trip.

In his office, Dr. Olladashi got right to work with bandages and antiseptic. Esteban took Hackenbush aside. "I watched," he said. "I could not stop it."

"It's okay, Esteban, I... I was lucky," she said. She was also crashing from the adrenalin high.

"How do you know such a man?"

"Bob? The white guy in the nice suit?" She

went on at his nod. "I knew him when I was young and confused and he was just as stupid as he is now. He owed some very bad people money and I helped him get away from them. That's not why he stopped the beating. He stopped it because he was in the mood to stop it, and we were lucky."

Esteban looked like he was going to say something but Dr. Olladashi interrupted whatever it was. He nodded urbanely to Hackenbush and turned to Esteban. "This man needs a hospital, and I need your help convincing him to go to one."

They disappeared into the treatment room. Hackenbush looked in and found all three of them— Dr. Olladashi, Esteban and Maria—waving their hands around. She caught Petey's eye and waved. He looked away from her. She figured this was as good a moment to leave as any.

Hackenbush stood in the hall and jiggled the keys in her pocket. The building was as unnervingly quiet as ever as she made her mental inventory of who was where at that moment. "Well, I guess it's now or never," she thought and headed for the stairs and the fourth floor.

The keys opened the door with the filing cabinets. She took a quick look in the other, larger room: it was full of dusty desks. This suite was similar to the suite on the third floor, just less inhabited and the file room was bigger. One bank of fluorescent lights was on, enough to see, but not enough to make her think anyone was coming back. She opened the top drawer of the nearest file cabinet; it was empty and so were the next two drawers. But the bottom drawer was full of cash. Hackenbush got nervous; she'd watched too much "Dragnet" and "Adam 12" on TV. Taking a Kleenex from her coat pocket, she wiped the stuff she'd touched and used it to open the rest of the file drawers. A few more had stacks of money, some pristine, some in wadded bales, but more cash than Hackenbush had ever seen in one place. "What the fuck is all this?" she asked herself. In the last drawer she opened, in the cabinet next to the hall door, there wasn't any money; there was a yellow backpack and big marble ashtray with black stains on it. Hackenbush had a hard time swallowing as she dug a wallet out of the backpack, a plain brown leather wallet with Tim Jackson's California Drivers' License and an ATM card in it. She put them back in the bag and picked up a raggedy paperback of "You Can Negotiate Anything."

"I was hoping..."

Hackenbush should have jumped out of her skin when Kevin spoke, but she didn't, she just looked up from the book at him, standing in the doorway to the outer office. He looked like shit. "Hoping what, Kevin?" she asked. She stood up and slung the backpack over her shoulder and picked up her tote bag.

"Hoping you wouldn't find that," he said quietly. "Or this." He looked completely beaten as he waved at the open file drawers of money. Hackenbush had left the bottom file drawer of each cabinet open.

She stood up and shoved the nearest drawer closed with her foot. "Did you know Tim was reading 'You Can Negotiate Anything'?" she asked, also closing the next drawer with her foot as she advanced on Kevin. "Isn't that sad? He was trying to learn your ways, Kevin, and he ended up in a non-negotiable situation." She side-kicked another drawer shut. "Because, like you said the other day, honesty and hard work don't pay off anymore." Another drawer slid home. "Have they ever really paid off? Don't guys like Bob, and his pal Miguel, and Boesky and God fucking knows who else get all the spoils." Another drawer. "And you and I just pay taxes and suffer." She shoved another drawer closed. "But we're alive and Tim is dead. Why is that, Kevin? Is this great country of yours and Reagan's so fabulous that an honest man is killed because he knew too much?" She stood in front of Kevin, who shrank back a little from her.

"He never found this," Kevin whispered. "I didn't kill him... I liked him, if things had been different, he could have become an agent here at Monroe, I–"

"Who killed him?" she asked. "Bob? One of Bob's thugs?"

"No. It was Gary. In a rage." Kevin met her eye. "But Mr. Jones's people helped us get rid of the body."

Hackenbush sighed. "I'm taking this for his family," she patted the backpack. "You're in over your head with Bob and his friends, Kevin."

"I know." Kevin snapped out of his funk a little. "Will you go to the police?"

"Later tonight. What choice do I have?" she asked, preparing to knock him down and run if necessary.

It wasn't necessary; they froze at the sound of the stairwell door being savagely slammed and then pounding footsteps in the hall. Hackenbush and Kevin took a step back from each other: Hackenbush into the file room, Kevin in the disused office area. Their interrupter bypassed the fileroom door and ripped open the outer office door. Hackenbush prayed it wasn't Gary, or Bob, but the voice that yelled, "Kevin!" was 100% female. Kevin got the hare in the headlights look on his face and Hackenbush figured it was time to split. She thanked her lucky stars and whoever Kevin's girlfriend was as she slipped out into the hall, away from the female bellowing in the office. She did catch the words, "... and you left the coffeepot on in the kitchen!" as she gently closed the door behind her.

Although no one on the fourth floor could hear her for all the one-sided yelling, she went quietly down the stairs. The lobby was deserted, but she found Esteban in the parking garage. "How's Petey?" she asked on her way by.

"Dr. Olladashi took him to Good Sam." Esteban looked hard at the yellow backpack, but didn't say anything. "Did you see Ms. Gonzaga?" he asked.

"No. She's here? When did she get here?" Hackenbush asked as he followed her to her car.

"About ten minutes ago," he said, looking worried. "She looked awful mad, almost crazy."

"Was she looking for me?" Hackenbush asked, opening her car door.

"No."

"Good."

She drove straight home and called Anna at the office, hoping she was working late. "Anna, what's up with Gilda Gonzaga?"

"I tried to call you, but all I got was the Monroe answering machine," Anna said. "I showed those computer files to Gilda; she found other files for insurance policies Monroe couldn't even write insurance for. She hit the ceiling and–"

"And went to confront Kevin," Hackenbush said, realizing she'd missed her chance to meet the fabulous Gilda Gonzaga. "Anna, I think you should call her and get her out of there."

"Why?"

Hackenbush told her what she'd found on the

fourth floor, omitting Tim's backpack, which was on the couch next to her.

"Oh my God, Hackenbush, I'll call you right back."

The phone clicked in Hackenbush's ear. She'd barely taken her coat off when Anna called back to say there was no answer. "Well? Gary Monroe killed Tim Jackson in the office and Bob's thugs dumped his body in the park. What do you wanna do? Anna? Anna?!"

"I'm here, Hackenbush," Anna said, sounding exhausted. "I don't exactly know, I think we should wait until tomorrow–"

"Anna, we have to call the police, don't you watch TV? That's withholding evidence, accessory after the fact," Hackenbush said, seriously. "Joe Friday would kick the shit out of us."

"Don't joke! I don't know what to do," Anna said, with tears in her voice. "Hold on, the other line is ringing. ... I'll call you back, Hackenbush, it's Gilda; the police found Gary's body in the park. I'm going to the morgue with her." She hung up without saying good-bye.

"I can't believe he went into the park. God damn, why does anyone listen to Bob?" she asked herself as she hung up the phone. Hackenbush realized this was now a two murder situation and she was in potentially bad trouble. There was one man in the world she could count on in a situation like this and she had to look up his number in the phone book.

Samuel Lowe was playing scales on his trombone and thinking about what he might want for dinner. He knew he'd never make a living as a musician, but to stop playing seemed worse than death; it was a living death, and he was too manly to give into that.

At that moment, all Sam had on his mind was embouchure, intonation, and getting through these last sets of scales. He was so intent, and it was after business hours, so he let the answering machine pick up. Of course he lunged for the phone when Hackenbush came on the line. "Hey, Hackinahackinahackinbush!... Yeah, I remember the Tim Jackson thing Anna asked me to look into... You did what? ... Could this be a joke?... No? .... You're not kidding? ... Okay, okay, um... Come over? Okay, good thinking... Yeah, I can pick up some Indian food at that place on Sunset... You'll call it in? Great, great... yeah, I'm on my way." At least his dinner plans were settled. Hackenbush hadn't sounded too freaked out, but she might be in shock. Samuel emptied the spit valve on his horn, took it apart and put it away.

Sam lived on the West Side, but he was on a mission to save his Hackenbush, so the Indian food take-out was waiting for him when he arrived, the lights on Sunset, and the traffic on the freeway were with him. He waved off Hackenbush's offer to pay for the food and admired her deft table setting and the no-nonsense way she dished up dinner.

"Are you really telling me you removed evidence from a crime scene?" he asked, glaring at the yellow backpack. "Can you tell me why you did that?"

"Because it seemed like a good idea," Hackenbush said, trying to brazen it out. "And I don't want Tim's family to suffer. Or something."

"You mean in the course of the investigation of Tim's murder, which you just complicated three hundred fold?" Sam asked. "I mean, thank you for leaving the murder weapon there at least."

"Okay, I know it was stupid–"

"Yeah, but you did it," he said, matter-of-factly.

"Now we just gotta deal with it. When I talk to the police, I'm leaving your burglarize–"

"I didn't!"

"Well, okay, I'm leaving that out, just going to say you found the money and the blood stained ash tray in the file cabinets," Sam said, getting up. "You stick to your story, but if you get hauled in, call me and don't say a word until I get there with a lawyer. Get it?"

"Got it."

"Good."

Samuel used Hackenbush's phone to call his friend in Rampart Police Station, who was on vacation but hooked him up with Officer Owens, who was on duty that night. They made an appointment to meet at the station on West Temple Street. Sam told Hackenbush to sit tight, he might need her to come down to the station, and to keep quiet about all this.

"Anna knows everything you do," Hackenbush said.

"Hope she doesn't do something stupid," Sam said, pulling on his jacket.

"Like what?" Hackenbush felt she should defend her friend.

"Like... I don't know. But I didn't know she was going to put you in so much danger."

"Well... y'know, Sam, I never felt I was in danger," she said. "I felt kind of sorry for them."

He patted her shoulder. "Why don't you play some music and relax, doc? This might not get started until morning, no sense worrying about it until then."

Hackenbush hugged him and said she really didn't know what she'd do without him. Samuel hugged her back, wishing he didn't have to meet Officer Owens, but duty called and he must be strong.

She took his advice, played her favorite Coltrane records until she felt tired enough to sleep. Shorty called to gossip, and that took her mind off her troubles. There was no way she was going to tell Shorty what was going on, and besides, Sam had it under control. At least she dearly hoped so. No one else called her that night.

"You look like shit, Anna." Hackenbush tossed her timecard on Anna's desk and sat in the guest chair across from her.

"Well, thanks," Anna said, scooping up the time card. Whether the thanks were for the neatly filled out timecard or sarcasm was unclear. "And good morning to you too. I didn't get a lot of sleep last night." Anna patted her flat and disheveled hair.

"So?" Hackenbush, well-rested and well-breakfasted, tried and failed to put some sympathy into the word. She lit a cigarette and offered Anna one.

Anna took a sip of coffee and accepted the smoke and the light from her guest. She coughed a little on the unfiltered Pall Mall, but then felt better for the higher-than-usual nicotine content. "So, I got to see our morgue again," she said, picking a shred of tobacco off her tongue. "Our morgue is a quaint brick building over on Mission by County Hospital not too far from your place in Lincoln Heights. Then I got to wait around Rampart for a few hours while Gilda tried to find out what the hell happened to her nephew. Then she cracked and I took her home. That's why I look like this."

"Sorry. What can I do?"

"Nothing. Although you might have to talk to the police about Monroe Insurance and what you saw there," Anna said glumly. "Gilda sent her lawyer over this morning to officially fire Kevin, she unofficially fired him last night, and the police were already all over the place with a search warrant when the lawyer got there."

"Really?" Hackenbush put on her most innocent face.

"Yes! Really! Any idea who called them in?" Anna asked with a well-bred snarl.

"Samuel Lowe."

"Sam? You called Sam?" Anna sat back and frowned. "How remarkably smart of you, Hackenbush, I wish I'd thought of that."

"Of the two of us, I was the only one who knew how much trouble we were potentially in." Hackenbush stubbed her cigarette out. "I figured Sam would know what to do and how to do it. Seems so, no?"

"Seems so, yes," Anna said, rubbing her temples.

"Anna, how did Gary die?" Hackenbush asked.

"He was shot. That's all I know."

The phone rang and Anna asked Hackenbush to talk to Dina Lee while she took the call.

"Are you okay?" Dina asked.

It was obvious to Hackenbush she was trolling for more information, so she just nodded her head and looked serious.

"That's two guys killed at that place," Dina continued, looking distressed. "That's crazy."

"Well, I think they won't need any more temps, if you're worried," Hackenbush said, watching Anna's closed door.

"I– I'm not worried." Dina fidgeted with a pencil.

Hackenbush hated to see women fidget; annoyed, she looked away from the younger woman.

"I just feel bad, y'know? I met Tim, he was a nice guy, and..." Dina trailed off and grabbed a Kleenex from the box on her desk.

Overcoming her annoyance, Hackenbush sighed. She didn't have a maternal or sororal bone in her body, so she couldn't put her arms around the kid and comfort her. So, in her book, she did the next best thing. "Dina." She looked into the girl's red rimmed eyes. "What are you working on these days?"

"Here?" Dina asked, and pulled herself together. "Dancing."

"Oh... a few things," she said, and proceeded to speak normally, even hopefully about her art and its practice.

Hackenbush listened and made encouraging noises until Anna opened her door and waved her back in. "Well?"

"That was Gilda," Anna said, sounding angry. "The police found nothing at the Monroe offices. They finally let her lawyer in and he found nothing–"

"What? Did they look on the fourth floor?"

"Yes. Nothing, Hackenbush, no money, no ashtray; nothing you said you saw–"

Dramatically placing one hand on her temple and holding up the other one to forestall Anna, Hackenbush closed her eyes and said, "Don't tell me, Kevin has vanished as well."

Anna blew out a breath. "Exactly."

They eyed each other over the desk, neither dared speculate on what might have happened if Gilda Gonzaga hadn't gone charging in: Gary would still be dead, Hackenbush was fairly sure of that. He was pretty far gone as it was.

Opening her deep desk drawer, Anna took our her purse and looked Hackenbush right in the eye.

"I'm going to see if I can get my hair done at one of the salons around here," she said, getting up. "This day is bad enough without looking bad."

Hackenbush followed her out; they parted company in the parking garage. From a payphone nearby, Hackenbush called Samuel and asked if she could come over that afternoon. He said he'd be delighted and would even give her lunch at his place. She said she'd be charmed, and, after she hung up had a terrible pang of conscience that she was going to completely ruin his lunch. She went up to her place, got the backpack and headed across town, arriving Chez Lowe just as lunch was being served.

"Oh, Sam," Hackenbush said putting her empty plate in the sink. That plate had briefly contained perfectly poached salmon and a green salad. "If I ate like this, I'd live forever."

"You'd have to quit smoking, too," he said, shoving an ashtray under her already lit Pall Mall. "To what do I owe the honor of you driving all the way across town?"

"I wanted to thank you for handling the mess at Monroe Insurance and helping me and Anna," she said, picking a shred of tobacco off her tongue.

"Not much to handle, if as you say, they cleaned the joint out last night," he said coolly.

"Yeah, well, I have one last favor to ask you."

Sam didn't say, "I knew it!"—he was too well brought up for that—he just said, "Oh?"

"Tim's backpack is in my trunk," Hackenbush said. "Would you please give it to Ross for the family and explain the whole thing to him?" She waited for the pained look to leave Sam's face and went on when it didn't leave. "Please? You see, I'm not the right person for this. If I do it, it will be ten times more traumatic than if you do it. And he'll yell at me for the same things you yelled at me for."

"I didn't yell at you, Hackenbush."

"You were yelling inside," she said, laying her hand on his. "I could tell. But Ross, he doesn't hold back." She smiled weakly. "And, y'know Sam, I just don't want to talk about it or think about it anymore. I mean, you're right, I was in danger and I was stupid to be there, and I'm trying really hard not to be really angry with Anna for sending me there, and angrier with myself for going there or staying there and going to the fourth floor. I just want to forget it and get on with my life."

Sam said he'd take care of it and got Tim's backpack out of her car. He met Ross the next day, gave him the backpack for the family and laid out the whole mess and why there was no murderer to put on trial anymore. Sam finished his spiel and waited for an explosion that never came. Ross didn't yell, he just said, "Thanks," took the backpack and walked away.

A few weeks later, towards the end of the third set at the Lotus Room on Saturday night, a young black man came in and sat at the end of the bar where Hackenbush couldn't miss him. She sang "Wave," "There Will Never be Another You," and "Mack the Knife," which they faked their way through because she added it to their repertory on the spur of the moment. Ross was annoyed, Cody stunned, Phil panicked, but Shorty was delighted. Then they played the break tune, which they knew really well.

Hackenbush strolled up to the man sitting at the end of the bar. "You clean up real nice, Petey."

"I never really fooled you, did I?" he asked.

"Sure you did," she assured him. "Did you fool

Esteban and Maria?"

"I fooled Maria, but Esteban was in on it," Petey said. "He had to be, he's illegal."

"You lie, Petey, I saw his paperwork," Hackenbush said, furious. "He's as legal as I am."

"Maybe," Petey sighed. "But if he's deported he'd lose everything here by the time he gets it sorted out. It's just easier to work with us when we ask." He showed her an LAPD badge; his real name was Curtis DuMar. She didn't think it suited him.

Hackenbush took a deep breath to keep from throwing her Ramos Gin Fizz in his face. "Where's Esteban now?" she asked, wondering what kind of bastard terrorizes a helpless man in the line of duty.

"I've no idea," Petey said. "I'm not here officially, I'm here to return the favor." He waited until she was settled on a barstool. "You screwed up a big investigation, Hackenbush, and now Gary Monroe's mother and aunt are raising hell about his murder, mainly that it's not being investigated. This is embarrassing the department, it's bad enough we look like fools to the FBI and the DEA, but having two shrieking crazy women on my boss's backs, that's getting real old real fast."

"Then investi–"

"It's pointless, Hackenbush," he said, grimly. "Some crazy in Macarthur Park shot Gary, like some crazy bashed Tim Jackson's head in. We were after bigger fish."

Hackenbush kept her mouth shut about Tim. "Like what?"

"South American drug lords," he said. "Since Ollie North and the Contras got busted by Congress, there's a lot of cocaine in LA right now. The rumor is North was funding the Contras with coke money from the U.S. Military planes bringing in tons of coke to airbases and selling it wholesale."

"Oh, come now." Hackenbush didn't resist rolling her eyes.

"Well, maybe not exactly like that, but something like that, because there's just too much coke on the street," DuMar who had been Petey said. "Gary was coked-out, but Kevin was stupid. We were really hoping his half-assed money laundering scam would net some big fish for us. Instead, you stumble in and tip off his boss, and he runs. Or he's dead, I don' t know, he might have served his purpose."

"Sorry." Hackenbush wasn't sure what she was apologizing for, but she thought she should.

"Not yet," he said. "You will be, though, if you don't find a way to get Gilda Gonzaga and Greta Monroe, their lawyers, and their friends in high places off my bosses' asses. The department is very embarrassed, Hackenbush, we hate that, we might have to haul you and everyone you know in for questioning. You might be okay, but how would it be for your drummer, your bass player and that little guy you dance with?"

"Now, wait a min–"

"Hackenbush, how long have you lived in this town?"

"A long time."

"Then you know what can happen," he said, finishing his drink. "I can't help you, and I was never here tonight." He walked out and didn't look back.

Hackenbush used the phone in Tanaka's office to call Anna. As it was after midnight, she woke her up and demanded she get her in to see Gilda and Greta the next day. There must have been something horrible in Hackenbush's voice because Anna didn't argue, she just said, okay, she'd call her with the details in the morning.

Hackenbush put on a severe navy blue dress and matching pumps. Usually she softened the dress with a witty scarf or string of beads, but not that morning. That morning she opted for serious over charming, convincing over persuasive, and relentless over diligent. There was too much at stake and she was too angry to be nice. Exactly whom she was angry with, she couldn't say, and sincerely tried to figure it out on her way to meet Anna and the Gonzaga sisters at the Temporary Insanity office.

It wasn't a very big office and Anna was the only one in it when Hackenbush arrived. "Okay, where are they?"

"I need to know–"

"You need to know what, Anna?"

Hackenbush's voice was so cold Anna just stared at her for a few moments. "I need to know what's going on," she finally said. "Gilda's helped me a lot and–"

"And what would you sacrifice for her?"

"Hackenbush, what the fu–?"

"I'll tell them what's going on," Hackenbush said. She strolled over and looked out the window at the empty Sunday Wilshire boulevard below. "And you can be there." She turned and looked at Anna. "Otherwise, I split, and ask Samuel to track them down for me." In some ways she wished she'd thought of this first; Anna tagging along was just going to be dead weight.

Anna stared back at her for a few seconds and then looked at her wristwatch. "Well, okay, Hackenbush," she said. "One car or two? They're expecting us at noon."

"Bitch," Hackenbush thought, but said, "One car." She might have to drive Anna home after this interview.

Anna parked her 1983 Toyota Corolla on a peaceful street off 8th near Highland and they trudged up a long path set in a perfect lawn to an imposing front door set back in an atrium-like structure. At least that's what Hackenbush thought it was, but just to be on the safe side, she asked Anna while they waited for someone to trek to the door and let them in.

"Yes, I think it's an atrium," Anna said, looking a little nervous. "This is Greta Monroe's home; I've never been here before."

A tall, slim lady with a nimbus of perfect gray hair opened the door. She looked them over with her dark blue eyes set wide apart in a face so faintly lined, only fatigue and sorrow made the lines show at all. She was wearing wool slacks and a matching cashmere sweater that would have cost Hackenbush a month's pay if she had it to spare and had slim enough thighs to dress that way.

"Gilda, this is Mabel Hackenbush," Anna said politely.

"A pleasure to meet you, Ms. Hackenbush," Gilda said, her voice calm and low. She stepped over the threshold and shook hands. "Anna has told me so much about you. Please come in."

Hackenbush suppressed the urge to say, "Lies, all lies," about whatever Anna had said. This was too serious and Anna really did have a high opinion of her. She hoped she still would when this was over. The other thing that crossed the Hackenbushian mind was that Gilda had greeted her outside the house, so if she had to, she could get rough inside it. She'd stood next to Hackenbush to size her up; she was a few inches taller, but lighter and less substantial. At least that's how it seemed to Hackenbush; she had a feeling Gilda was afraid of her.

"Well, maybe she should be," Hackenbush thought, as she and Anna followed Gilda through lovely rooms with hardwood floors, stained glass windows and intimidating portraits of old, stern looking men who could've lost a few pounds. Exiting a pair of French doors, they crossed another immaculate lawn and went into an all glass building. Hackenbush couldn't decide if it was a hothouse or a conservatory and gave up on it when they came to Greta Monroe, sitting in a wheelchair next to a space heater cranked up to full-blast. She was a smaller version of her sister; Hackenbush couldn't tell which was the elder.

It was already hotter than hell in the place; Hackenbush's glasses fogged up a little. She shrugged off her jacket and was glad she wasn't wearing more clothing. She accepted a seat and a glass of ice water from Gilda, but declined the splash of scotch. She had nothing against scotch drinkers or getting started at noon, it was Sunday after all, but she needed a clear head and only liked single malts anyway.

"I believe you knew my son, Miss Hackenbush," Greta murmured so low Hackenbush could barely hear her.

"Yes, I did," Hackenbush said over the space heater fan. She glanced at it and Greta turned it off. "I didn't see much of him because he was all strung out on cocaine, I think, and he wasn't in the office very much."

There was a shocked silence that brought a nice glow to Greta's pale cheeks. "That's quite an accusation," she said coldly.

"Oh, c'mon, Mrs. Monroe, let's tell each other the truth," Hackenbush said. She reached for her cigarettes, but thought better of it in that overheated, stuffy room. "There's a lot at stake here. You and your sister and your minions harassing the LAPD about his murder is going to hurt a lot of living people so you can feel good about one dead one."

"Hackenbush!" Anna hissed at her.

"Harassing the LAPD?" Gilda cut in. "Only to do their job."

"Yeah, well, that would be great, but you're stirring up a hornet's nest, Ms. Gonzaga," Hackenbush looked over her shoulder at her. "You screwed up a long-term, potentially huge LAPD surveillance operation they were hoping to catch some mid-sized drug dealers with. The kind of people, not too far up the foodchain, but far enough to need their cash laundered and Kevin was just the guy to do it for them. When you marched in and said whatever you said to him, the whole mess blew up and the LAPD was left with nothing. Worse than that, they had the FBI and the Drug Enforcement Agency watching them work without a net. And when they fell, they really crashed. They're embarrassed they couldn't nail an amateur like Kevin and a few minor drug lords. Adding injury onto insult, you and your sister are nagging them to solve a murder that, in their minds, is less solvable than Tim Jackson's murder."

"What do you mean?" Gilda asked.

"Gary went into the park and was shot, right?" Hackenbush asked and got a nod. "If they could trace the gun, they would have already. If they could find the guy who did it, they would have. After all, to all appearances, Gary Monroe was a respectable white guy. He was just in the wrong place at the wrong time, and the person who killed him has vanished into the swarms of homeless burn-outs and crazies in Macarthur Park."

"But there must have been witnesses," Gilda persisted.

"Either they're too fu– messed up to know what they saw, or they're more afraid of the police than whatever they live with in the park," Hackenbush said, wishing she didn't have to explain this. "You haven't been around that office a lot lately have you, Ms. Gonzaga?"

"No, our business is mainly in Century City now," she said, looking tired. "Gary... Gary wanted to be on his own."

"So you put in him charge over the guy who'd been loyally with you for nearly thirty years," Hackenbush said.

"Kevin was... efficient," Gilda said slowly. "And–"

"He was more than that, Gilda," her sister said suddenly, and turned to Hackenbush. "My husband hired Kevin and he helped build that office. He was a good man for many years."

"Was." Hackenbush sighed. "But about a year ago he started money laundering for drug dealers, mid-size, but mean ones, and I think he was keeping Gary strung out so he could loot Monroe Insurance in peace."

"But why, Miss Hackenbush?" Greta said after a tense silence. "That's what we hoped you could tell us."

Hackenbush shifted her gaze to Gilda. "You were going to close that office," she said. "I suspect that neither Kevin nor Gary wanted to move where they would be under your thumb. I further suspect Gary got strung out and that's how Kevin got to know the drug money people."

"That doesn't excuse–" Gilda began.

"No, it doesn't excuse a thing. However, it's what I think based on what I saw," Hackenbush said. "I also saw file cabinets full of cash and a marble ashtray with dried blood on it and Tim Jackson's backpack, which made me think he was killed in the office and then dumped in the park."

"What?" Greta asked slowly. "What do you mean?"

Hackenbush looked into Greta Monroe's sad face, and decided to lie to her. "What I said, Mrs. Monroe. Someone killed Tim in the office, hid the murder weapon and Tim's yellow backpack, and dumped his body in the park, or had it dumped there," Hackenbush said slowly. "I don't know who, there were some thuggish types around; some of them beat up an undercover police man in your parking garage one night. But it might have been Kevin or Gary because Tim discovered something they couldn't let anyone else know, or maybe Gary asked him to get him some drugs in the park and Tim refused." She paused to let that sink in. "I think that because Gary took a swing at me when I refused to do it."

"Hackenbush..." Anna was shaking.

"It's okay, Kevin rescued me. I think he regretted, too." She patted Anna's hand and locked eyes with Gilda, who, knowing the whole story, was looking guilty and relieved that Hackenbush had made some attempt to spare her sister's feelings. "I bet you think Kevin bolted."

"I do." She seemed to welcome the change of subject.

"It's possible he's dead," Hackenbush said calmly. "Looking back, he was in way over his head. He might have become too much of a liability for the drug guys. Or he might have run with their money, but they'll catch him, and when they do, they'll kill him."

Greta Monroe was motionless in her wheelchair, staring at her hands folded in her lap. Gilda kept her eyes down, but her lips were compressed and drained white in barely contained rage or tears or both. Anna looked nervous and tired, very tired. Hackenbush let out a sigh and forged on to the real reason for her visit. "And now, I need your help," she said pleasantly, like she was addressing a gardening club. Three pairs of eyes widened at her, but she was undaunted. "The LAPD can't solve Gary's murder, but they can destroy everyone they can get their hands on in the process of not solving it, while getting you two off their back by appearing to work on it. I've been threatened and warned about this; that's why I'm here. They'll haul me in for questioning and toss me into the Sybil Brand jailhouse as a material witness for as long as they want. Then they'll get Anna, her staff, her temps, Tim's widow, his family, the guys in my band. We're not rich people, Mrs. Monroe and Ms. Gonzaga, we don't have money for lawyers, we can't miss a week of work without serious financial consequences. And I'm not as tough as I look; I wouldn't last long in Sybil Brand. Neither would Anna, and my band..." She looked at her hands and made fists. "One jail fight for my drummer, bass player and guitarist, and they couldn't play for weeks, maybe months, maybe never. My dance partner, I don't even want to think about what would happen to him in lock-up." Hackenbush paused to take a breath and get her voice back under control. "So, you see, ladies, I came here to ask you to please let Gary's murder alone," she said, searching Greta's face for some sign of comprehension. "I know you loved him, and I wish he was alive to get some help, but he's not, and a lot of innocent people are going to get hurt by the LAPD in an investigation they've already given up on except for whatever pressure you're putting on them. So, I'm here to ask you to let it go," she said. "I'm here to beg you, if that's what it takes."

To Hackenbush, the silence seemed to go on forever, but eventually Greta Monroe cleared her throat. "I leave these things to my sister," she said softly. "If you'll excuse me..." She reached over and turned the space heater back on.

On cue, the three ambulatory women left the glass house and went silently back the way they came. At the door, Gilda stood looking across the threshold at them. "We'll do what you ask, Miss Hackenbush," she finally said. "Enough damage has been done."

"Thank you, Ms. Gonzaga," Hackenbush said simply.

Gilda returned her thanks with a nod and closed the door.

Anna asked Hackenbush to drive them back to her office. On Wilshire, Hackenbush noticed she was crying. "Hey, Anna?"

"I don't think Tim's death really hit me until now," she stuttered. "It's so unfair, his wife and their baby, it's so wrong he's dead."

Anna's car was an automatic, so Hackenbush reached over and held Anna's hand. "I know someone else who got hurt in this mess," she said.

"Who? You? Are you-?"

"Strangely   enough,   I'm   okay,   Anna,"

Hackenbush said, giving her hand a squeeze. "And if Gilda does what she said–"

"She will! She keeps her word," Anna snapped.

"Good, good, then everything will be okay," Hackenbush said, glad Anna was pulling herself together. "There was a guy who worked in the lobby of the Monroe building, a really nice guy named Esteban. I found out last night that he was being blackmailed by the police, and he ran when the police poured in. No one knows where he is now. I feel sad about that. I never knew Tim, but if you say he was a great guy, then I agree with you. But I knew Esteban a little and I hope he's okay, wherever he is."

"Do you pray, Hackenbush?" Anna asked, wiping her eyes.

"No."

"Then I'll pray for Esteban for both of us."

Hackenbush kept her eyes on the road and didn't say anything. She was taking inventory: Gary and probably Kevin were dead, and Gilda Gonzaga's lawyers and accountants were going to have a mess to sort out. Tim Jackson was dead, and his little girl would have to grow up without him. Esteban Morales was alive somewhere and she hoped he was okay. She was filing them away; a cold, but necessary job. Otherwise she'd be swept away by sorrow and horror. People die or are destroyed every day in Los Angeles; it's either tragic or stupid or both, and the worst part, for Hackenbush, was that there was nothing she could have done for any of them.

The End

Ginger Mayerson lives in Los Angeles, California. She's published in the Coe Review, Roux Magazine, The Velvet Mafia, and The Journal of the Image Warehouse. Originally trained as a composer, she now writes novels, essays, reviews, interviews, makes collages, edits the Journal of the Lincoln Heights Literary Society, and publishes books and magazines at the Wapshott Press. You can find the Hackenbush scene at www.gm.wapshottpress.com. Or you can get more on Mayerson at www.GingerMayerson.com.

Other books by Ginger Mayerson

Dr. Hackenbush Gets a Job

Dr. Hackenbush Gains Perspective

Dr. Hackenbush Gets Some Culture (Storylandia 8)

Electricland

The Pajama Boy

Darkness at Sunset and Vine

www.ingramcontent.com/pod-product-compliance
Lightning Source LLC
Chambersburg PA
CBHW070926130626
46555CB00001B/305